# THE FIRE ESCAPE

WHITNEY JOHNSON

*Tyra,*
*congrats on winning*
*the giveaway!*
*Happy reading!*
*Whitney*

*Edited by*
SUSAN GAIGHER

# CONTENTS

# 1

Lisa Doyle, the head nurse at Lakewood Residence Center, walked up to the reception desk where Margie stared at her computer.

"Mr. Nelson is still not responding, poor guy. His dementia keeps getting worse." Lisa glanced up from her chart to see Margie chewing the cap of her pen. "Margie?"

"Hmm?" Margie's bright red hair hung perfectly straight down to her shoulders, flyaways matted down by hairspray. She'd left the top button of her green cardigan open, revealing a precise shirt collar underneath.

"Did you hear me?"

"What?"

"Mr. Nelson..." Lisa looked at her, wide-eyed.

"Yeah, poor guy," Margie replied, shaking her head with sympathy.

Lisa made a habit of stopping by Margie's desk to fill her in on all the residents. Lakewood was home to sixty residents, ranging in ages from fifteen to eighty-four. All residents had mental disabilities, including Down syndrome, autism, dementia, and Alzheimer's. That is, all residents but one: Peter Doyle.

Peter was the resident Margie had been thinking about all morning, but she didn't want Lisa to know that. Lisa was the fifteen-year-old boy's mom—and that was the problem. Margie may have just shattered Lisa's world.

"Are you all right?" Margie asked.

For someone so obsessed with outward appearances, Margie thought it was ironic that today—of all days—Lisa was wearing scrubs with so many wrinkles they looked like she had left them sitting in the dryer overnight. Her short, bobbed hair was knotted and, looking at the circles under her eyes, Margie wondered if she had slept in her makeup.

"Yeah, I'm fine."

"Just checking," Margie replied with a smile.

"All right, well, I better get back to work." As Lisa was walking away, she added, "Make sure I never use that pen."

Margie took the pen out of her mouth and threw it in the trash. She was not in the habit of chewing her pen, but she was so nervous about today she didn't even realize she had the pen in her mouth until Lisa said something. She wheeled her chair as close to her desk as she could, then checked the time. She couldn't sit still. Her foot tapped on the floor, fingers drumming on the desk as she kept looking toward the entrance for a visitor she was expecting.

It wasn't easy for Margie to lie to Lisa. The two of them had become close friends. At least, that's what Margie thought. They were hired around the same time—Lisa as a nurse, and Margie as a maid. It was Lisa who suggested to their boss that Margie be promoted to the reception desk—a job that might not seem prestigious, but Margie was really the gatekeeper of Lakewood. No one came in or out without her approval.

Though Margie was grateful for the promotion, she couldn't shake the feeling that Lisa had ulterior motives behind her manning the reception desk. There was something behind that sweet smile Lisa wore. And the visitor she was expecting any minute might just be the key to finding out what it was.

PETER SAT at the edge of his bed like he did every afternoon. His brown hair lay perfectly parted and gelled-down like his mom expected it to be, gentleman-like. His clothes, from Goodwill, hung baggily on him. He had worked for years to gain his mom's trust, and part of that work meant doing things he didn't like, like gelling his hair and wearing clothes that he was years away from filling out.

Lisa no longer locked his door from the outside, and with all the work Peter had done to build trust, leaving his room was out of the question today. His mom would be checking in on the patients that lived in his hallway. Peter followed most of his mom's rules, but to keep himself from going insane, he would often sneak to the reception desk to visit Margie, a trusted confidant. Although Margie was a good friend of his mom's, she had never told Lisa that Peter snuck out. Peter always appreciated that about Margie. In a tightly confined world, knowing that he could trust Margie meant a lot to him.

THERE WAS a buzz at the front entrance door and Margie checked the video monitor to see who it was. When she saw her friend, Angela, and a police officer with her, the thumping in her chest became overwhelming. *This is it.*

She opened the door, and Angela approached the desk.

"You really had to bring an officer with you?" Margie asked, sweat appearing on her upper lip.

"After doing some digging, I felt it would be the best way to approach this case, yes. This is Officer Halliday." Angela was very matter of fact, professional.

"But she won't find out that I'm involved, right?" she asked in a hushed tone.

"I will do my best to keep that promise." Angela handed Margie papers with legal documentation. "Now can you lead us to Lisa?"

Margie eyed the paper while slowly standing. "Right this way," she said, stepping out from behind the desk and leading Angela and the officer down the hallway. Every now and then she glanced back at Angela with hesitation, who only gave her a nod of encouragement.

"Lisa?" Margie asked as they approached her.

She was documenting in her chart and didn't look up. "Yeah?"

Margie cleared her throat and handed her the papers. "Sorry, her credentials check out."

"Oh, who's this?" Lisa studied Angela and the officer.

"They're from Social Services. This is Angela and Officer Halliday."

"Nice to meet you." She shook both of their hands. "Who are you here for today?" It wasn't uncommon for Social Services to visit Lakewood.

"That's what I was telling you." Margie pointed to the paper in Lisa's hand. "They're here for Peter."

"Here for Peter? Why?" Lisa questioned, shuffling through the papers.

"Ma'am, are you Lisa Doyle?" Angela asked.

"Yes."

"We are here to evaluate the living situation of your son."

"What right do you have?"

"We are following through on an anonymous report we received. We just need to look into a few things."

PETER TOSSED his baseball repeatedly in the air above him, letting it fall into his open hand. His room was decorated with legends from the field: Mickey Mantle, Babe Ruth, Sammy Sosa, and the most compelling, Lou Gehrig, who died from ALS—the same disease Peter's dad passed away from. The disease, nicknamed after the famous baseball player, Lou Gehrig, is what started Peter's obsession with baseball.

The posters were the only things adding color to his room, and his mom's way of trying to make Lakewood feel like a home to Peter. Which, of course, only worked for a time. There was nothing about living at Lakewood that felt like home. The smell of cafeteria food seeping through the halls, sharing a hallway with fifteen mentally-ill residents, some of which he had to remind every day who he was; even after living at Lakewood full-time for seven years, it still felt foreign to Peter.

He counted the tosses of his baseball and wondered about life before Lakewood. *292, 293, 294.* He and his mom used to live in a town just a few miles away. Their home had been in a suburban neighborhood with lots of kids his age to play with. Then, that all got left behind. Like Lisa did on a few occasions, she brought Peter to Lakewood to spend the evening with the residents. He would join in their kickball tournaments, or call out letters and numbers for bingo. He would sleep in one of the guest suites and have breakfast with the residents in the morning before he went home.

But the last time he visited, it was different. Instead of Lisa picking him up and taking him back home, she came with packed bags to stay.

What Lisa had told him would be a temporary stay became permanent. Now, seven years later, he was confined to their small room, tossing a baseball, waiting for his mom to let him out like she would let a dog out of its kennel.

*314, 315, 316.* He stopped. Raised voices coming from the hallway piqued his interest. Curious, he tiptoed to the door and cracked it slightly to peek down the hall. Through the small opening, his green eyes focused on something that surprised him. It was his mom, beside a police officer and a woman—both with arms folded, cornering Lisa against the wall.

*Who is that woman? And why is there an officer?* He closed his eyes and leaned his ear forward as if to heighten his sense of hearing.

"Well, I don't really see how that is any of your business," Lisa said defensively, hands on her hips.

"Ma'am," the woman said, putting one of her palms out as if to calm Lisa. "We are following protocol. Just tell us where your son is so we can gather the information we need."

"And if I don't?"

"Then we will have reasonable cause to remove him from your custody without questioning."

Lisa's eyes narrowed. In defeat, she pointed down the hall. "Last door on your left."

Peter stepped back from the door, fearful he had been

spotted—not by the strangers, but by his mom. He paused for a second before hurrying back to the end of the bed. The words the woman had said lingered in his mind. *Remove him from your custody?*

His fingers curled around the baseball, the grooves of the stitches indenting his hand. The door creaked with each knock from the officer until it was ajar enough for him to poke his head through the opening.

"Peter? I'm Officer Halliday. Can we have a word with you?"

Peter stared at the officer, his eyebrows furrowed, not knowing how to answer.

The officer invited himself in and motioned the woman to pull up a chair from the corner of the room. She strode across the wooden floor; the room was dimly lit by lamps and the January winter sun shone through the closed window. She sat in front of Peter, only an arm's length between them, then gathered her papers in her lap and gave Peter an encouraging smile.

"Peter, I'm Angela. I work for Social Services."

Peter had seen others from Social Services at Lakewood plenty of times. Many of the residents were minors that were being looked after. However, he had never encountered them himself. In fact, for the last seven years, unless a person worked or lived at Lakewood, Peter didn't have any contact with them. Ever.

"I don't want you to be nervous. We only have a few questions for you, okay?" She looked him in the eye with a soft, unobtrusive gaze. Her blonde hair spilled over her shoulders.

Peter looked wary, but nodded.

"Can you tell me when you first moved here, Peter?" She motioned her hand around the room as she asked. She looked around, probably taking note of the room's simplicity; a bed, a nightstand, and a small dresser were all that occupied the space, along with a corner kitchenette that housed a refrigerator and microwave.

"I was eight."

"And what happened, to make you move here?" She had a way of asking questions in a non-accusatory tone. She was gentle, polite.

"My mom told me we lost our house. We couldn't afford to live there anymore."

"When you were eight? And how old are you now, Peter?"

"Fifteen."

"Does your mom ever talk to you about leaving Lakewood?"

"I used to ask, but I don't anymore. She doesn't like to talk about it."

Angela jotted a note in her folder.

"So she has made you continue living here?" Her blue eyes penetrated through the frame of her glasses.

"I guess," he said, his hands beginning to sweat against the baseball.

"What do you do here at Lakewood? What's your daily routine?"

He looked back and forth between the two of them, not sure what they were fishing for. "Um...My mom usually wakes me up for breakfast. We eat here, in our room. Then she leaves to go work her shift and I wait for her or another nurse to come get me."

"Come get you for what?"

"It depends. Sometimes I play the piano for the residents."

"Do you do that for fun?"

"I guess it can be fun, but I really only do it because I get paid to."

"Like a job?"

"Yeah, they didn't want to hire someone to come each day, so my mom volunteered me. It at least gets me out of this room."

The officer let out a deep exhale and shook his head. Angela continued writing in her folder.

"Do you spend a lot of time in this room?"

"Pretty much all day."

"Why don't you go down to the lake, or into the dining hall with some of the residents?"

"Oh, mom would never let me do that alone. She said it's too dangerous."

"Why is it dangerous?"

"She said that some of the residents here could get violent and attack me. Sometimes if another nurse is available to protect me, I get to go to the activities room and play games with them.

Angela glanced at the officer with a disapproving look and Peter knew he had said too much. He wondered how much trouble he would be in later when his mom found out.

"But at least each day I have tutoring," he blurted out. Peter hoped Angela couldn't sense his nervousness.

"And when you say tutoring, what do you mean?"

"Mom hired a teacher for me so I can do my schooling here. I use some of my piano money to help pay for that."

She looked up at Officer Halliday again. "Do you like your schooling?"

"Sometimes. But I really just miss school. I miss having friends."

Angela continued asking questions. Peter keenly felt

that he was under observation; he couldn't help fidgeting with his hands as he was asked questions about his mom. He carried on explaining how he longed for a normal life outside of Lakewood, why he was here, and why he couldn't go to a normal school. Angela listened intently, all the while jotting notes in her folder, until they had finally reached the end of their visit. In a calm voice, she told Peter that he would need to gather belongings he wanted to take with him.

"Take with me where?"

"Peter," she said, looking into his eyes, "We are going to take you to a lovely home for the next two days while we ask your mom a few things. We need to understand why she has made you live here for so long, okay?"

Peter looked at her with both relief and apprehension. He wanted to know why he was here too, but he didn't understand why he had to be separated from his mom to do so.

"Why don't you get some clothes and a toothbrush," she said, beginning to walk to the door before adding, "And why don't you bring your school books with you too."

Angela and Officer Halliday left him to gather what he wanted. He wasn't sure how to pack, but he stuffed some clothes and books in a bag. Then he went over to his night-stand and picked up his Lego figurine that was dressed in a baseball uniform—his friend he named Lou. It was the one thing Peter had from his childhood home. Nervous to walk out of Lakewood for the first time in seven years, he took one last glance around his room; his baseball heroes stared back at him. Leaving Lakewood was something he had dreamed of for years. He just wasn't leaving the way he thought he would be. With his Lego friend in his hand, he sighed and opened the door.

Angela was waiting for him in the hallway. As they walked toward the exit, Peter saw Officer Halliday with his mom.

"You can't take him from me!" Lisa screamed. She held her stance well until she saw Angela with Peter. She tried to run for him, grab him, keep him with her, but the officer held her back. "No! *Peter,*" she sobbed. Her short, thin strands of hair plastered her face, sticky from tears and sweat.

Peter stopped walking, frozen with confusion. *They said it would be two days. I'll be back in two days.* But seeing his mom screaming, tears streaming down her face as she tried to push past the officer, he began to wonder if maybe they were wrong.

Angela bent down and whispered in his ear, "It's time to go, Peter."

With a soft push on his shoulder, she led him through the exit.

The doors flung open and they descended the steps.

Lisa kept wailing, "Don't take him from me. Please..." She seemed to lose strength as the doors began to close.

Peter turned back and took one final glance at his inconsolable mother before the closed doors blocked his view. The last thing he saw was her sliding down the wall onto the ground, Margie embracing her as she sobbed.

Out in the parking lot, the cold winter afternoon was silent, but Lisa's screams echoed in Peter's ears. Angela led him to her car and opened the passenger door for him. Without saying a word, he sat in the passenger seat, his eyes glazed over. Of all the times he had imagined leaving the hospital, this was definitely not how he pictured it. His dreams of a joyous exit had turned into a nightmare.

The ride was quiet. Angela tried to keep up light conversation, but Peter was not in a talking mood. Peter looked down at his Lego friend still in his hand. Then, closing his grip around Lou and turning toward the window, he let a single tear run down his cheek.

PETER JOLTED awake to the sound of his mom's screams. He had been having recurring dreams about the day he was taken from her—six weeks earlier. The investigation on his mom was still ongoing; Peter got an explanation from Angela that she was not fit to have him in her care right now.

"What do you mean?" Peter asked.

"Well, we don't know everything definitively. So, for now, we need to keep you here at Elaine's." Elaine was his foster mom.

Peter didn't push for more information. He wasn't sure if he wanted to know what they had found out about his mom. Obviously something was going on if he was still in foster care.

He stared at the luminescent clock. The neon numbers read 2:38. Peter turned on his side and looked at the shadows cast by the streetlight. He hummed to himself to get the noise of his mother's screams out of his head, but with the sound of wind whistling against the window, he wasn't having much luck.

Every night he awoke from his nightmare, he had to reorient himself with the surroundings in his room. To his astonishment, each time he was at Elaine's—that, to his relief, wasn't a dream. Peter let his rhythmic breathing calm him. The repetitive in and out helped him clear his mind.

The thumping in his chest slowed, and he got out of bed

to change his shirt, which was completely soaked through with sweat. The light outside his window burst into a star as tears pooled in his eyes when he yawned. He watched as the points of the star jutted in different directions, and he couldn't help but think his heart felt the same way—pulled in different directions, tugged by guilt and relief.

Now wide awake, his mind flooding with questions about his mom, he slowly opened his bedroom door and tiptoed down the stairs to the kitchen. It had taken him weeks to feel comfortable leaving his room without permission.

The first week at Elaine's, he would wait for Elaine to come and get him, just like he had at Lakewood. He was so used to being confined, and under the control of his mom, that the prospect of leaving his room made him nervous. It took a lot of coaxing, but with tenderness, and the help of therapy sessions, Elaine eventually convinced him that he did not need her permission to come out of his room. Still, being the middle of the night, he wanted to make sure he didn't wake Elaine.

As he made his way down the dark stairway into the kitchen, his bare feet swished against the linoleum floor. He shuffled to the cupboard and pulled out a glass. Then, setting it on the counter, he opened the refrigerator door and poured himself a glass of milk. The light from the inside of the fridge illuminated the room as he put the gallon back on the shelf. While the fridge was still closing, he turned back to the counter and spotted a shadowy figure sitting on one of the barstools. He jumped back, startled.

"Oh gosh," he said, holding his chest. "How long have you been sitting there?"

"For about a half hour." It was Elaine.

Widowed for nearly a year, Elaine was lonely. She had

kept the house that she and Larry—her husband—had lived in for the entirety of their marriage, but now, with her three children married and living in three different states, she was lonely.

She moved to the wall and flipped the light switch. They both squinted until they adjusted to the light. "So. How ya doing, kiddo?" Her hair was pulled up into a high bun, her grey roots showing.

"Fine," he said before taking a gulp of milk.

Elaine gave him a reproving look. "Are you sure?" She hesitated before adding, "I heard you stirring in your room."

"Yeah, I'm good." He knew he should just tell Elaine what was going on.

She waited.

He contemplated what he wanted to say. In the last six weeks, he had grown close to Elaine. She felt like a grand-mother to him. She and her home engulfed Peter with love. Within the first week, Elaine somehow managed to get a picture of him and frame it as if he were her grandchild. He had his own room. His baseball heroes appeared on the walls. A comfortable mattress and pillows welcomed him at night. The only thing haunting him was his dream. The recurring dream. A dream that relentlessly replayed reality.

Peter cleared his throat. "I keep having a dream about the day they took me from my mom. Over and over I see her curled on the floor sobbing, screaming. And when I wake up, her screams echo. They fill my head and I have a really hard time shaking them."

Elaine put her fingers over her mouth, seemingly thinking about what to say. Her eyes sagged; she looked exhausted. "Is it every night?"

He shook his head. "No, luckily not every night. But I'm

definitely having them more often." He shrugged his shoulders then added, "I just hope they'll stop soon."

"I think it would be best if we mentioned this to Angela. Maybe she will know what to do."

He didn't want to admit it, but he knew Elaine was right. He felt awkward mentioning these dreams. In his mind, he was too old to be having nightmares.

"We'll talk to Angela when she comes in the morning, okay?"

Peter nodded.

"All right then, let's go get some sleep." Elaine squeezed his shoulders then nudged him up the stairs. She followed one at a time to go easy on her arthritic knee.

# 2
---

The next morning, Elaine knocked on Peter's bedroom door to inform him that his tutor would be at the house any minute. Angela had expressed that she thought it would be good to keep Peter's schooling routine while he was adjusting to living with Elaine.

It seemed to Elaine that despite wanting to go back to normal school, Peter was grateful to continue with his tutor for the time being. She suspected he was still getting used to the sudden free will he had in foster care. At least, more so than he'd had at Lakewood. Angela had mentioned that several kids she oversaw thought foster care was restrictive and deprived them of their agency, but it was likely that Peter, not having had any independence at Lakewood, felt free.

Angela made visits every few weeks to observe and make sure Elaine's home was a safe place for Peter to be. While Peter and his tutor worked in the kitchen, Elaine and Angela sat in the living room.

"How is Peter doing?" Angela asked.

"Pretty good. He has made improvement. He doesn't wait

in his room until I come get him anymore. We've made it over that hump. And he is opening up a bit more. I think he is starting to realize that I am someone he can trust. At least, I hope he knows that."

"That's great. Are you noticing anything strange in his behavior?"

Elaine, somewhat overwhelmed with the responsibility to make sure she met every need of Peter's, was grateful to have Angela as a sounding board.

"Sometimes I hear Peter stirring at night; he's having trouble sleeping. He woke up in the middle of the night last night, and told me that he's having recurring nightmares about the day he was taken from his mom. He said her screams fill his dream and they echo as he wakes up."

Angela frowned. "How often is he having these dreams?"

"He couldn't pinpoint exactly, but he said in the last couple weeks he's had them more often."

Angela made a note in Peter's file. "Do you know if Peter has mentioned this in therapy?"

"I'm not sure, but I don't think so. Last night was the first time he mentioned the dreams to me. I'm worried that he has bottled it up inside."

Angela kept making notes in Peter's file as Elaine stared out the front room window. She had thought about Peter's schooling several times, but never had the courage to bring it up before now.

"Angela? Do you think maybe changing Peter's routine could help him?"

Angela's face scrunched in inquiry, so Elaine elaborated.

"I was thinking that it would be good to immerse Peter into the school system." Elaine watched Angela's face as she went on, trying to gauge her reaction. "I think it would be good for Peter to start meeting kids his age. Give him someone to relate to."

Angela put her pencil to her mouth. Then she waved the pencil up and down while pointing it at Elaine and said, "You know, I actually think that's a great idea. And now would be the perfect time." She got excited, and her foot, which she had been sitting on, suddenly popped flat onto the floor. Sitting up straight, she added, "It will be the last term of the school year, so he will only have to endure it for a couple of months. If it doesn't seem to be helping, we can have him homeschooled again."

"I'm relieved you feel that way," Elaine said, relaxing.

"That day we took Peter from Lisa was...difficult to say the least—even for me. I think school would be the perfect thing to pull his focus elsewhere."

Elaine watched as Angela flipped through the contents of her bag, apparently pleased when she pulled out her iPad.

"Now there are four high schools nearby, so I'm just going to verify which district you would be in."

"That's pretty incredible. When Larry and I moved in, there was only one high school. It's hard to believe how much this town has grown."

"And it keeps growing," Angela added as her fingers plunked on the screen. "Here it is, Dalesprings High School."

AFTER PETER'S tutoring session ended, and they waved goodbye to his tutor, Elaine and Angela asked Peter to join them in the living room.

"Peter," Angela started, "Elaine and I were talking, and

we both feel that the time is right for you to start public school."

It was something Peter had wanted for years, but now that the opportunity was here, he could feel his nerves rising. "Right now?"

Elaine nodded. "I think it would be really good for you, Peter."

"I'm afraid of what the other kids will think of me."

"Well, I don't see why they will think anything," Angela assured. "You'll be starting fresh, and the kids will think you just moved here. I don't think you'll need to worry."

"Yeah, but what if kids start asking questions? I can't just tell them I grew up in a mental institution."

"You don't need to tell them that, Peter. This is your experience, your time in school. But if it will help, you can tell people you came to stay with your Aunt Elaine for a while."

Elaine chimed in. "She's right, Peter. You don't owe them any explanations. If you don't want them to know where you grew up, then you don't need to tell them."

When he dreamed about going back to public school, it was because he longed to make friends, he wanted to be normal. But now, even after six weeks at Elaine's, he didn't feel normal. If word got out about where he grew up, he could only imagine the conclusions people would jump to, of what they would make of him. Then who would want to be friends with him?

"Everything will be okay, Peter," Angela told him.

"We'll take this week to prepare, okay? I'll even take you shopping for some new clothes," Elaine said excitedly.

Peter wasn't excited to go shopping, but he did agree to start public school, even though the thought of it made him nervous. "All right."

WITH HIS MIND on starting school, Peter was able to sleep through the next several nights without his nightmare. The morning of his first day of school, he was awake before his alarm went off. He lay flat on his back with his hands under his head, staring at his white textured ceiling and thinking about the last time he had been in a public school. He had been in elementary school, third grade. He was a naturally social kid with many friends.

Lakewood had never given him the chance to be social with people his age, so jumping straight into high school made him nervous. One thing he was sure of was that it would be very different from his elementary days, especially because he didn't know if that social kid was still inside him —at least, with kids his age. His best friend at Lakewood had been Kenny. He was ten years older than Peter and had Down syndrome. Peter loved everything about Kenny. In a world where Peter had felt trapped, Kenny was a boost of positivity. Every time Kenny saw Peter, he would stop whatever he was doing so he could run to him and embrace him in a tight hug. He listened to Peter as he taught him about his baseball heroes, made him smile when he was sad, and loved Peter unconditionally, even when his own mother did not.

One of Peter's dreams about leaving Lakewood was to go back to public school. Now that the opportunity was here, the prospect of socializing with other kids was frightening. What would he tell people? Could he tell them he was in a foster home? That he had just been taken away from his mom? Could he tell them that he was secretly happy to be in foster care? He couldn't tell them where he grew up or he would be the weird kid. Then there would be all sorts of questions—about the patients, why he grew up there, what was it like, was *he* a patient, why did he get taken from his mom, on and on.

With all his thoughts rushing through his head, he made the resolute decision to follow Angela's advice. If asked, he would tell people he was staying with his "Aunt Elaine" for the rest of the school year.

The morning cold made him shiver when he got out of bed. It was that time of year when you blasted your heater in the morning, but had to use the air-conditioning in the afternoon. The foliage of the trees was covered in morning dew. The sun pierced through the peaks of the mountains as it began its morning rise.

Since arriving at Elaine's, Peter felt a sense of calmness, of freedom. For the first time in years, he wasn't constantly looking over his shoulder in fear of his mom. Before Social Services arrived, his dream of leaving Lakewood always included Lisa. He had never expected that being taken from her would make him feel so relieved. It made him realize that through all these years, Lakewood might not be what he needed to be free from; it was his mom.

HIS MOM USED to be his whole world. She had been his everything. She had cared for Peter in a way that every mother should—comforting him when he missed his dad, playing with him, tucking him in every night. She loved him.

Peter thought that would never change, but with each passing year at Lakewood, Lisa seemed to lose her maternal instinct. She was no longer soft-hearted, patient, loving. She was stressed, manipulative, and controlling.

The first time he saw her at a boiling point was when he was ten.

"Mom, it's been two years. When are we going to go back home?" Peter asked.

"Peter, we've talked about this. We are not going back to that house."

"Well, maybe not that house, but can't we live in a normal place?"

"We don't have the money for that."

"Just a small apartment?"

"Peter, that is enough."

"But—"

She turned around so fast that Peter barely had time to duck before the plate she threw smashed against the wall behind him. "I am not going to ask you again. We are *not* leaving Lakewood, so stop bringing it up."

Wide-eyed, he laid on the floor, his heart pumping so fast he could feel his ears beating.

Shocked by what she had done, but not apologetic, she walked out of their room and shut the door behind her.

Peter was left on the floor, looking at his arm where a ricocheted shard of glass had cut into it. He rinsed his arm off in the sink, grabbed a towel, and cleaned up the rest of the shattered glass.

AFTER GETTING READY, Peter sat on his bed, bracing himself for the school day ahead. He mentally told himself that he could get through this first day of high school. Endurance was something he had learned at Lakewood. Instances of him asking about leaving Lakewood before his mom threw the plate always ended with the same repeated phrase. His mom would crouch down and look him straight in his eyes. Then, she would gently take Peter's arms in her hands, ensuring she had his attention, and say, "Just hang in there one more day."

*One more day.*

Those words flooded his childhood, and Peter eventually realized that "one more day" meant day, after day, after day. Until the days abruptly stopped with the visit of Social Services.

*What did my mom do?* Peter thought. It frustrated Peter that he was being kept in the dark. Angela wouldn't tell him the details, only that there was a situation that made his mom unfit to be his guardian right now.

When he heard pans clanking in the kitchen, he realized he had been lost in thought and quickly made his way downstairs, where he could smell the breakfast Elaine was cooking.

He still couldn't believe Elaine cooked him a hot breakfast every morning. It was so much better than the cafeteria food he used to eat at Lakewood. He sat on the stool across the counter, facing Elaine.

"Oh, well you sure look handsome!" Elaine enthused. "Were you able to find anything you liked in your closet? We can always take things back if we need to."

"That's okay. I like the clothes." Peter had worn Goodwill clothes for the past seven years, so anything new was more than appreciated.

Elaine's dimple appeared as she smiled to herself, which made Peter smile in return. He could feel the happiness within her spread, and he knew it was because she was happy to have him there. He could tell she liked having the company.

~

JUST LAST YEAR, Elaine had lost her husband, Larry, to pancreatic cancer. When he was diagnosed, Elaine dropped everything to take care of him. Her passion from a young age was horticulture. She was always drawn to plants and wanted to know everything about them. Eventually, her curiosity led her to become a horticulture professor. And though that was her passion, Larry was the love of her life and she would have done anything for him to still be by her side. He had battled for years with chemotherapy and radiation, but the cancer metastasized and took over several organs before Larry passed away. Burying him was the hardest thing she had ever done.

People say you shouldn't make any rash changes within the first year of a loved one dying, but toward the end of the year, Elaine couldn't take the loneliness anymore. Her kids were busy raising kids of their own, and though she received calls from each of them regularly, most of her time was spent by herself, in her empty home.

It was wonderful having family in town to support her when he passed, but one by one, each of her children went back home and left her alone in the empty house. With each month of the silence, she felt it was time to bring something new into her life.

One evening she sat, as she always did, reclined in Larry's chair in her living room. It was her way to feel connected to him. While working on her new hobby of cross-stitch, the local news broadcast on the television. She had picked up cross-stitching to pass the time, but didn't know how long she would be able to keep it up, as she needed not only her reading glasses, but also a magnifying glass to see where her needle was.

"*This is a statewide concern that many children are in need of a home, and there are not enough foster parents to place them with,*" the woman on the television said.

Her fellow newscaster spoke next. "*Many of these children are malnourished and in desperate need of a loving family. If you feel like fostering a child is something you could do, please call the number on your screen.*"

Elaine put down her magnifying glass and set her cross-stitching on the side table. Before she could think, she grabbed the pad of paper and pen sitting by the lamp and jotted the number down.

The next few days followed the same routine as she walked into the living room several times and looked at the number she had scribbled down. One time she thought if she just turned the pad of paper over, the thought would leave her. Besides, how was she supposed to take care of a child? She was getting too old for that.

After three days of mental debates, she found herself dialing the number to find out how she could help. Within a month, she was approved through Social Services and set up to be a foster parent. She just never expected her first kid would be her perfect match.

WHILE ELAINE CONTINUED TO COOK, Peter walked to the sliding glass door adjacent to the counter. Looking out at the backyard, Peter couldn't help but feel sad. Plants were overgrown and misshapen, their limbs out of sorts from not being pruned. The grass was tall, with dandelions poking through every few inches. Vines outgrew their trellises. Peter deduced that no one had set foot in the backyard in years.

He had grown used to the beautiful grounds of Lakewood that his room had overlooked. He used to spend hours staring out the window, longing to be out on the lawn or under the big oak tree. At Elaine's, he noted it was the opposite; her yard was terrible, but because he felt so welcomed inside, maybe he had no need to be out there.

Elaine set two loaded plates in front of each bar stool. When she saw Peter staring at the backyard, she explained, "There was no time to worry about the yard when Larry became sick. That yard used to be my pride and joy. Now I just don't even know where to start."

They ate in silence. Peter glanced out the door every so often, still taking in the yard monstrosity. To Peter, Elaine had been a perfectly organized and put together person. Somehow the disarray of the yard helped him see the human in her, the imperfection. She had been Peter's personal superhero, and he found it hard to see the shortcomings of a person he had put on a pedestal.

ELAINE HAD Peter get in her 1970s Chevy pick-up to take him to school. The drive was a slow one with Elaine carefully maneuvering the streets to avoid children who may run out in front of her. Although Angela and Elaine had registered Peter for school, Elaine felt it necessary to accompany him to the office for his first day.

She pulled into the visitor parking and the engine rumbled as it turned off. She turned her head toward Peter, her hand still on the gear. Now that they'd arrived, Peter could feel the blood drain from his face.

"Peter?" Elaine said. He didn't answer. "Peter?" she said again as she placed her hand on his shoulder.

"I feel sick."

"Oh, kiddo, it'll be okay. You just have to walk in there and be yourself."

"That's what I'm afraid of."

"What do you mean?"

"Well, all these kids—I'm sure most of them, anyway—have been in public school their whole lives. They know how to make friends."

"Some of them," Elaine responded. "But there are going to be so many kids in there that feel unsure of themselves. That's what high school is. Some kids may be more confident, but deep down they're just trying to figure out who they are in the world."

"But I just feel like I'll stick out, and not in a good way. I've had such a different childhood, and—"

"Then you have so much more to bring to the table." She looked him straight in the eye. "Peter, you are one of the best kids I have ever come to know. Who cares if you grew up under different circumstances? That place you grew up in..." She motioned with her hand, waving it in the general direction of Lakewood. "It taught you how to have love and compassion for others. That will go a long way here." She pointed at the school.

Peter looked up at her compassionate eyes and succumbed. "Okay, let's go."

Dalesprings High School—home of the Tigers—was named after the city and was positioned in the middle of the valley. The oldest school in the district, Dalesprings hosted a student body of eighteen hundred kids.

Peter and Elaine walked through the front door and

watched as students made their way, some in no hurry, to their classes.

"Ah, there it is," Elaine said as she lightly swatted Peter's shoulder. She pointed to a sign protruding out of one of the walls; it read "Office." They headed toward it.

As they walked, Peter watched the demeanor and body language of the students as they interacted with their peers. If Lakewood had made him anything, it was observant.

He was so used to the plain colors worn by the residents and nurses at Lakewood that the vibrant clothes the students were wearing really stuck out in his mind. The students dressed with a statement, wanting to be heard through the way they appeared.

Some students walked together, but didn't say anything, their eyes focused on their phone screens. Living virtually seemed more important than reality. Peter understood the need to escape reality, but he had never done that with a phone, just with stories he would make up in his mind.

The one-minute warning bell rang, and students began to scurry through the halls to their classes. In a matter of seconds, the classroom doors closed, leaving the hallways still and empty.

The office staff took advantage of the quiet and began guiding Peter through his schedule. After brief instruction, they thanked Elaine and let her know they needed to take Peter to class.

Peter turned to say goodbye to Elaine, and was surprised to find that she looked almost as nervous as he felt. She grabbed Peter by the shoulders and encouraged him again.

"Just be yourself, Peter. That's the best person to be." She gave him a nod then left him in the office.

The thing about being *himself* was that Peter didn't know who that was. He'd lost all sense of who he was under the control of his mom. He'd barely thought for himself under that roof, and now he was supposed to be...*what?* He wasn't sure.

The school secretary stood up from behind her desk. "Peter, I'm going to give you a tour of the school real quick to get you oriented, and then I'll drop you off at your first class. Sound good?"

Peter nodded.

The school was laid out in a simple grid. Classrooms were labeled easily enough, with their hall letter followed by room number. It didn't take long for Peter to catch on. Evidently secure in the knowledge that Peter could find his way around, the secretary dropped him off at his first class.

"All right, here is Mr. Jensen's English class. He is one of the favorite teachers at the school."

The comment made Peter relax a bit. He was grateful to start off with a teacher the other students liked.

"If you need anything, please ask," she said before taking her leave.

THE SQUEAL of the door being pushed open turned every head in the class. Peter felt his cheeks flush as all eyes stared at him. He wanted more than anything to leave and pull the door closed again. Mr. Jensen perked up from behind his computer and quickly stood to greet him.

"What can I help you with, young man?"

"I have this class, sir," Peter said, then added, "I'm new." He felt dumb.

"All right! Well, welcome. What's your name, son?"

"Peter."

"Great. Come on in." Now standing in front of the class,

he invited Peter to join him. "Why don't you tell us a little bit about yourself."

Words started to spew out of his mouth. "I live with my Aunt Elaine. She'll be taking care of me for a while. I'm not sure how long I'll be able to stay, but I hope it's a long time." His cheeks felt like fire.

Mr. Jensen didn't seem to notice his nervousness. "Well, we are glad to have you while you're here. Why don't you take the seat in front of Karen. Karen, raise your hand." Mr. Jensen gestured to the indicated desk. The kids watched as he took his seat and the metal legs clanked with the desks adjacent his.

He sunk down, hoping he could shrink enough to not be noticed for the rest of class. Mr. Jensen spoke. "Peter, your timing couldn't be more perfect. I just split the class into pairs for the term project and we had an uneven number of students. Now we can split the threesome."

Two of the three girls looked up in frustration. The third didn't seem fazed.

"Who is willing to break the group?"

Without hesitation, the third girl raised her hand. "I will," she said.

"Perfect. Jeddie, your new partner is Peter."

The frustrated girls sighed in relief that they were not pulled out of the group. Jeddie gave Peter a polite wave.

"So," Mr. Jensen continued, "Let me explain what the project is, and then you can pair together for the last ten minutes of class." Peter got more nervous as Mr. Jensen began explaining. He was starting to regret his decision to come to school.

For the last term of the school year, each student was to get to know their partner, like *really* get to know their part-ner, and come up with a creative project to present them to the class. Mr. Jensen was expecting more than surface-level facts about the students. He really wanted them to dig deep and find out something intriguing.

"The project should be well thought out and articulated since it is the project for the entire term. Any questions?" Mr. Jensen asked.

Peter became nauseated as he thought about letting someone know him as well as Mr. Jensen was hoping. This project was the exact thing he had been hoping to avoid.

To Peter's relief, questions about the project ran long, and before they could break off with their partners, the bell rang to excuse classes. Peter shuffled his notebook, shoved it in his pack, and zipped it closed as he walked out of the class. His face flushed red as he scurried through students and made his way to the bathroom. The hallway near him quieted as everyone made their way to their next class while he hid in a stall and waited for the hallway to empty. He waited, like he was so used to doing. For just a moment, he wished he was back at Lakewood, in the confines of his comfort zone.

## 3

Jeddie Sams was sitting in the lunchroom with her friends, her long, brown hair draped behind her shoulders as she held it back to eat. Most days she used her time at lunch to relax and be with her friends, but today, she couldn't help but think about the new kid she had been paired with for the term's project. From where she sat, she could see the opening of the lunchroom where Peter stood, looking unsettled. It had been the second time she had seen him that day. She tried to catch him after Mr. Jensen's English class, but his exit had been too abrupt for her to be able to find him in the crowded hallway. She hadn't been able to talk with him then, but she was eager to meet him now.

Although she tried to never single anyone out, the nervous boy from class that morning intrigued her. Something drew her toward Peter. She was used to meeting new students who came to the school, but Peter's demeanor was different from other new students. Yes, most new students were nervous, but it was something else.

When Mr. Jensen was explaining his expectations for

their school project, she started to jot notes about her first impressions of Peter. He looked so out of place. Other new students always seemed nervous, but Peter looked terrified. There was something different about him and she wanted to find out what was underneath the wall that he was putting up.

She got up from her seat to approach him, but was beat by Karen Graham, a girl from their English class.

"Hey there. I'm Karen. You were in my English class this morning." Karen played with her hair as she spoke and blushed a little. Jeddie was embarrassed for her.

"Hi," Peter replied. He barely made eye contact.

Karen touched the back of his arm and motioned Peter toward where she was eating lunch with her friends. Jeddie watched them walk away as she stood planted where she was.

She expected this from other girls as Peter was pretty attractive, but that wasn't what drew Jeddie to Peter. Still, she was annoyed with the way Karen was flirting with him, and caught off guard by her own sudden attachment to him.

Back at her table, she watched Peter and only realized she was staring at him when she and Peter made eye contact. She tried to look away, but she couldn't help herself; every time she tried to focus elsewhere, her gaze was pulled back to him. By the looks of it, she was making him uncomfortable, and was grateful when the conversation at her table pulled her out of her trance.

"There's a baseball game this Friday, are you all planning on going?" Jeddie's friend, Natalie, asked. Dalesprings' baseball team had won the state championship six years in a row. The Friday night games had become a town event.

Jeddie loved school games. She loved the camaraderie of it all—people coming together from all walks of life. She loved watching new friendships blossom, even if those friendships only lasted the duration of the game. She would listen to the older generation reminisce about their old teams. She'd watch the players blushing when they saw their girlfriends in the stands, and their girlfriends fluttering with excitement when their boyfriends stepped up to the plate to bat. She loved all of it.

Her friends agreed that they'd be at the game and began making plans to hang out afterward. She glanced back in Peter's direction, but he was gone. She was glad to see Karen was still at the table, meaning Peter had gotten away, but wondered where he had gone. She scanned the lunchroom until she spotted him.

Her lips formed a smile when she saw that he was sitting with a special needs student. She watched in amazement as Peter seemed to completely relax. He was a different person than that shy, tense boy who was in her English class that morning. Peter and Marcus were laughing and high-fiving, and Jeddie's desire to get to know Peter grew stronger as she watched.

WHEN THE BELL rang to go to class, she got up to leave the table and glanced over to where Peter had been sitting. He somehow managed to slip away without her seeing him. She knew she looked idiotic, but she raised up on her toes, craning her head in all directions, to see if she could spot him. Then, without any success, she slumped down to flat feet.

"Who are you looking for?" It was her friend, Natalie.

"Huh?" Jeddie played dumb.

"I saw you staring at him through lunch. You got a crush on the new kid?"

"No, I'm just curious about him, that's all."

"Right."

"Honestly, Nat. I promise."

"If you say so."

"I do." Jeddie was resolute.

Natalie dropped the subject. "I've got to head to class. Maybe see you after?"

"Yeah. I'm headed to see my dad after school, but I'll look for you before I go."

BECAUSE JEDDIE WASN'T TERRIBLY good at math, she didn't care much for the subject. They were studying trigonometry and Mrs. Keel tried to make things more interesting by wearing a princess crown. On top of her head. Every Friday. She had a bucket of them at her desk and if she hadn't already put one on by the time class started, she asked the students which one she should wear. Beside her professional nametag on the door, there was a second one that read "Princess Keel." Some students might have thought it was weird, but Jeddie found it a bit endearing. She liked Mrs. Keel, and she appreciated that she cared enough to have a little fun.

Today, though, was not Friday, which meant a regular class period where time seemed to slow. With Peter in her thoughts, Jeddie drifted away from learning math to wondering what she could do to make her and Peter's term project fun. She thought the best place to start would be her favorite place—the nursery.

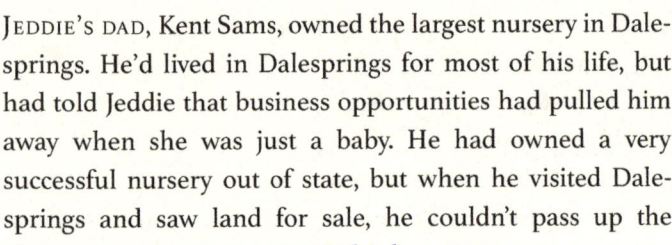

JEDDIE'S DAD, Kent Sams, owned the largest nursery in Dale-springs. He'd lived in Dalesprings for most of his life, but had told Jeddie that business opportunities had pulled him away when she was just a baby. He had owned a very successful nursery out of state, but when he visited Dale-springs and saw land for sale, he couldn't pass up the chance to open up a nursery in his hometown.

Kent grew up on his family farm and, for as long as Jeddie could remember, loved hard work. He had helped his mother with upkeep of their yard and his dad out in the orchards, which eventually led him to study horticulture and landscape design in college. It had been his dream to own his own nursery, saying that he wanted to bring beauty and life into others' yards. His passion for plants showed, and Jeddie had evidently inherited it. She loved being around the plants, loved seeing their growth and how they added beauty to the world.

When the Dalesprings nursery had first opened, Jeddie loved being in the greenhouses. There, she was able to prop-agate and transplant. She spent hours going from green-house to greenhouse, watering everything from the trays of small sprouts to baskets of blooming flowers. Jeddie would come out drenched from waist to toe, dirt all over her clothes, and her hair matted down because of the humidity in the greenhouses. It might sound like a miserable chore to some, but she loved every minute of it. She found being alone, watering in the heat, relaxing.

In her free time, she studied everything she could find about plants: when they bloomed, how tall and wide they would become, if they were a shade or sun plant. When she'd started to retain what she read, Kent let her walk around with customers. She would answer their questions and suggest plants they should buy for their home projects. When she had finished helping her customers, she would walk along the burlap-wrapped trees and find a hiding place by one of the trunks. She loved to close her eyes as the sun shone through the fluttering leaves, and hunker down, knowing perfectly well she would have mulch all down her backside when she got up.

With spring still on the cusp, however, she decided to hang out in the warmth of her dad's office today. She sank into the couch and, without meaning to, dozed off. She slipped easily into the cozy state right between being barely conscious and asleep. When Kent, who had been doing inventory at the front of the store, shuffled into his office, he plopped into the chair at his desk. The abrupt noise startled Jeddie awake.

"Oh, sorry, Jed, I didn't see you there," Kent said.

Scrunching her face and squinting, she stretched her arms above her head before propping herself up. Through a yawn, she said, "It's okay, Dad." She sensed his exhaustion and added, "How's your day been?"

"It's been good. Just getting ready for the busy season ahead of us." He was struggling to get his foot out of his tight work boot, and with a strong pull, he almost fell out of his chair when his foot finally broke free. "How about you? You have a good day at school?"

"Yeah. There was a new kid today. I got paired with him for the term's English project."

"What's the project?"

"It's a 'Get to Know You' thing. We have to find out as much as we can about our partner and then present them to the class in a creative way."

"That could be fun."

"Yeah, but I don't know how I'm going to get to know him if I can't even get to talk to him."

"What do you mean?"

"Well, there was something off about him in class. I couldn't figure it out, and then when the bell rang, he ran out of class so fast I couldn't catch him. Maybe it was just nerves." She sat up straight on the couch. "But what really might be the challenge is all the girls. Karen all but mauled him today in the cafeteria and stole him away to her table. It was annoying how she flirted with him."

Kent knew that even though Karen had been Jeddie's good friend in the past, her and Jeddie's personalities began to clash last year. Jeddie had always been outgoing and an innate leader. About the same time that Jeddie won the student council election was when she and Karen started having problems. While Jeddie was busy with her student council duties, Karen was even busier working to steal the attention of the student body. To Kent, it seemed like she was so jealous of Jeddie's new position at the school that in order to gain confidence, Karen worked on turning their group of friends against Jeddie. It didn't surprise him that Karen tried to take charge of the new kid as well. "Maybe you need to pull him aside and set up a time where the two of you can do your project outside of school. Why don't you bring him here after school? You can show him around the nursery and he can see what we're doing to get ready for spring."

"I'm glad you said that because I had the same idea."

"That's great. Any time you want to invite a friend, you are welcome to."

Jeddie got up and gave Kent a hug. She was grateful her dad somehow always knew what she needed.

**4**

I n the morning, Jeddie tracked Peter down at his locker. "Hi, Peter," she said as she approached him. He was glancing back and forth between his schedule and his books, evidently trying to decide which ones he should take with him. She wondered if having a whole new set of classes today was putting too much stress on him.

"Hi." He put his schedule in his pocket awkwardly.

"I don't know if you remember me. I'm the one Mr. Jensen paired you with for our project."

"Yeah. Jeddie, right?"

"Wow, I'm shocked you remembered my name."

"Oh." Peter's cheeks flushed red.

"It's a good thing. I guess I'm just surprised since you only heard my name once. My dad is good at that sort of thing, remembering names. It's like he meets you once and your name sticks forever." She could feel herself rambling.

Peter just nodded his head.

"So, should we exchange numbers so we can get together and start the project?" Jeddie asked.

"Yeah, that would be great."

Jeddie held her hand out for his phone and handed hers to him. "Why don't we just type it in for each other."

As she went to the contacts tab, she noticed only one phone number: Elaine. She tried to make it seem like she hadn't noticed as she handed Peter back his phone, but thought it was odd.

"How about we meet after school today? Then we can head to my dad's work. I think that's a good place to start."

"Sure."

The morning bell rang letting students know it was time for their first class.

"Well, if I don't see you before then..." She waved, turning on her heel and walking down the hall.

Jeddie let out a long exhale when she had put enough distance between them. She snuck a peek behind her and saw Peter doing the same thing. The conversation had evidently taken a toll on both of them.

AT THE END of the school day, Peter stopped at his locker again. He pulled out his phone and made a quick call to Elaine to let her know he would be late getting home.

When he hung up, he could see Jeddie bouncing down the hall toward him. She wore a smile as her hair flung from side to side.

"You ready?" she asked.

"You bet."

"Great. Usually I just walk to my dad's work. Is that okay? It's about six blocks from here."

"Sounds good. Lead the way." He was trying to act cool, but he was feeling conflicted. Intuitively, he wanted to tell Elaine he had changed his mind about school. On the other hand, he just wanted to make friends. He'd missed his friends more than anything else while in Lakewood. The project wasn't exactly the way he had imagined meeting new friends, but finally getting the chance to spend time with someone his age felt like the best day of his life.

Jeddie led him out the school doors and down the street. Maybe it was something inside the school that made them both act so awkward because now that they were outside on their own, conversation started to flow naturally. That is, until Jeddie asked the question Peter had been dreading.

"So, Peter, where did you grow up?"

Peter squirmed. Trying to answer honestly, but without giving details, he said, "Well, I grew up in a town called Mountain View. Just north of here."

"Did you like growing up there?"

He thought about how he could still answer honestly. "I liked it when I was little."

"Just when you were little?"

"I'm sorry. I'm not very good at talking about myself. Do you mind if we just focus on you today and maybe start with my story another day?"

He was relieved when she agreed.

The six blocks to the nursery was a brief walk. There were a few cars in the parking lot, but it was mostly empty. Noticing the big piles of different kinds of dirt each sectioned off by large cement barriers on the far edge of the parking lot, Peter was curious. "What is all the dirt for?"

"Customers buy it to put in their flower beds."

He must have been lagging behind a bit because Jeddie lightly tugged his arm and said, "C'mon. This way."

She led him through the main building. A woman poked her head out from a doorway when she heard them.

"Hi, Jeddie. I'd thought you'd be coming in about now. Who's your friend?"

"This is Peter. We're partners on a class project."

"Well, nice to meet you, Peter." The woman stuck out her hand to shake his.

"Peter, this is Heather," Jeddie explained. "She's worked here for quite a while. She's a good family friend."

"Nice to meet you, Heather."

"You taking inventory?" Jeddie asked her.

"You bet." Heather gave Jeddie a wink. It was an inside joke between the two of them, teasing about how much they loved inventory.

"Well, we'll leave you to it. I'm going to introduce Peter to my dad."

"Have fun." Heather smiled as they walked down the hallway.

They went into an area that was labeled *Employees Only*. Jeddie put her finger over her lip to warn Peter to stay quiet as they entered her dad's office in the back of the building. The room was lit by natural light from the windows and a small lamp attached to the desk where Jeddie's dad was sitting, working on a landscape design. As Jeddie tiptoed toward his desk in an effort to startle him, a floorboard creaked and gave her away.

"Hey, sweetie," her dad said without turning around.

Her plan now foiled, Jeddie slumped into the chair beside him. "Hey, Dad."

"How was your day?"

"Good. This is my friend, Peter, from school." She nodded her head in Peter's direction.

Not realizing anyone had come in with her, he swiveled around in his chair. "Now you, sir, could have actually star- tled me! You might have to give Jeddie some tips on how to make a quiet entrance." He nudged his daughter with his elbow. "Kent Sams. It's nice to meet you, Peter." Kent outstretched his hand and gave Peter's a shake. "What are you two up to today?"

"School project," Jeddie answered. "We have to follow each other around and get to know one another. I thought this was the perfect place to start."

"Yes, it is," Kent replied. Turning to Peter, he said, "Jeddie spends every afternoon here. She can't seem to get enough of the place. I think she gets that from me." He chuckled.

Peter pictured himself back in the confinements of Lakewood, yearning to be in the peaceful gardens just beyond his four gray walls and barred window. So often he had stared out the window, watching the residents enjoy the warm sun, walking the grounds, sitting on the dock by the lake that rested underneath the massive granite mountain. He remembered staring out the window, wanting to be in the warmth of the sun, while the chill of the dull gray room behind him ran down his back.

Before Lakewood, there had been so much life in his childhood room. It rang with vibrant, inviting colors. Pictures of his own design hung on the wall, looking down at an outer space bedspread and all his Lego creations. He loved his old home. Picturing his room at Lakewood, he could only see bland grays as if it was a prison cell.

Kent turned to Jeddie. "Why don't you take Peter down to the greenhouses. You can show him where all the magic begins. Meet me back at the house, say...5:30? We can all have dinner together?"

Peter surprised himself—and by the looks of it, Jeddie as well—by happily agreeing.

The gravel crunched under their shoes as they walked

the pathway that led to the greenhouses. According to Jeddie and Kent, in a few weeks, the nursery would be bustling with customers gathering plants for their spring projects.

Peter had expected the nursery to be loaded with plants, but as he looked around, the acres of land looked somewhat barren. As soon as they stepped into one of the greenhouses, however, he was in awe. Hundreds of trays covered the tables inside. Green sprouts peaked out from the soil where plants were starting to grow.

"This is where the magic begins," Jeddie said, motioning Peter to follow her. "These trays with the smallest sections are plug trays. We plant seeds so they will germinate." She walked over to a table where the plants were bigger than the rest. "It takes about three weeks for the seeds to grow to this stage. Before they grow much more, we transplant them to larger trays so the roots can expand."

"That's pretty cool. I've never seen anything like this." Peter looked at each of the tables with their small beginning sprouts. "So where are the bigger trays?"

"Come on, I'll show you."

They walked out the back door of the greenhouse, and Peter stood in astonishment. He couldn't believe how many other greenhouses there were. He counted at least fifteen when Jeddie tugged on his arm to lead him inside another greenhouse.

"This is the greenhouse I'm in charge of," she said.

"Really?"

She nodded. "Yeah. When my dad first bought this nursery, there were only two greenhouses—the main one I just showed you, and this one." Above them hung dozens of baskets with flowers billowing over the sides. Three long rows of tables had flowers blooming in more colors than Peter had ever realized plants grew in.

"I would spend hours in my dad's shadow watching how he meticulously cared for each of the plants. It was amazing to watch how those small seeds grew into plants like these.

"My dad was so patient teaching me, and I guess he could see how much I loved taking care of the plants along-side him. Eventually, as the nursery grew, and he became busier, it was hard for him to devote his attention to the greenhouses as he had done before. So, he asked if I wanted to take over. I watch over most of the greenhouses generally, but this one is all mine." She looked around, beaming with pride.

"This is amazing." Peter started to walk down one of the aisles. To him, it seemed to stretch for a mile. He ran his hand softly over the tops of the plants. It was refreshing to feel the new growth of leaves. "What made your dad open this place?"

"This is the second nursery he's owned. When we lived in Washington, he owned one there. He came out here for business and found this place. It was a dream of his. Ever since I can remember, my dad has had a passion for plants. He can take the worst yard, dream up a whole new one, and then make that dream a reality. It's one of my favorite things about him—getting to watch the design he creates on paper bloom to life."

"I wouldn't even know where to begin with something like that."

"It's not easy. He's the hardest working person I know."

"I bet."

"When we first moved here, this was an empty plot of land. My dad started small, but that small start gave him the edge to grow into the business the nursery is now."

Peter walked to the end of the aisle and turned to take it all in, feeling the last of his tension leave him. He closed his eyes and took a deep breath in. As he opened his eyes, he saw Jeddie watching him, smiling. Jeddie's cheeks burned red at having been caught, but he just smiled at her before they both let out a laugh.

"I really like it here," he said.

"I'm glad, because there's one more place I want to show you."

Jeddie led him out the back door of the greenhouse. He thought only one greenhouse lay perpendicular to the one they had just exited, but found out quickly that he was mistaken. When they rounded the corner, Peter was surprised to see three more greenhouses beside it. Jeddie kept walking toward what looked like a dead end. But on the other side of the last greenhouse, there was a gate in the fence that ran along the back side of the nursery.

He followed Jeddie through the gate.

"Welcome to my home," she said.

"Woah." Behind the nursery was a hidden oasis.

"This is my favorite time of year because of the way our yard looks."

The yard was immaculate. Peter had never seen anything quite like it. The grounds at Lakewood were beautiful, but this...this was above and beyond. A stone walkway trailed from the back gate to the built-in patio lined with cherry wood garden boxes. Plants Peter couldn't name filled the yard with precision. Trees of all shapes and sizes, shrubs, flowers, and grasses fit perfectly where they were. Tulips and daffodils bloomed, filling the yard with vibrant colors.

"Your dad did this?"

"Yeah. He landscaped the whole yard. It's one of my favorite designs he's ever done."

Peter's eyes followed the stone path that jutted in a different direction toward the back corner of the yard. It led to a giant oak tree, which Peter recognized as the same variety of tree he longed to sit under at Lakewood.

His eyes were pulled upward by the tree's impressive height. "Wow. That's really cool."

Jeddie followed his gaze. "It's better from the top. Come on, I'll show you."

At the base of the oak, stairs started and wound their way to the tree house up top.

"I think I'll just look at it from here," Peter said.

"What? Don't be silly, the view from up there is amazing. You have to see it."

"I just don't like being up that high."

Jeddie took his hand and started to climb. About halfway up, her brown hair bounced as she flipped her head to look at Peter. A quiet laugh left her lips, and he assumed it was because of how nervous he probably seemed.

"It's safe, I promise," she assured him, but he didn't say anything, too focused on his footing. "The view is worth it."

Still a little reluctant, he let her pull him to the top.

He dropped her hand when they both reached the balcony and held onto the railing with a tight grip. With a confident stride, Jeddie walked to the other side of the house.

Chipped, worn paint on the balcony indicated to Peter that she must visit that spot often. Sitting, she hung both legs off the side and rested her elbows on the railing.

"Isn't this the perfect view of the nursery?"

Peter hadn't looked out, still struggling to find his footing so high up.

"You okay?"

The skin around his fingers turned white with his tight grip on the railing. Beads of sweat formed around his temples and his tightly shut eyes.

"Mm-hmm," he lied.

"Here." She stood, gently coaxing him to keep shuffling to the edge of the balcony where she had been sitting.

Inch by inch, he made his way to sitting Indian style, backing away from the edge and leaning against the house for some stability. Jeddie plopped down next to him and dangled her feet off the edge once again.

"Don't you want to let your legs hang?" she asked.

"No, no. I think this is good."

"Are you at least going to open your eyes?"

"I'm working on it."

She smiled and patted him on the shoulder. "Whenever you're ready."

The breeze blew between them in the silence that followed. Jeddie decided to take his mind off the height.

"My dad built this for me a couple of years ago. It's just the two of us, so when he would work late nights at the nursery, I would stare out the back window of our house until he finally appeared around the greenhouses. I think it made him a bit sad that I was alone in the house just waiting. So, he built this tree house so I could overlook the nursery. It's just the right height, and this side faces the office at a perfect angle so I can see him the second he comes out the back door." She paused for a moment before continuing. "Do you ever get so sick of being around people all the time that you just can't wait for quiet moments by yourself?"

Peter thought about those agonizingly lonely days at Lakewood. "Well, I used to be alone all the time. So now I actually welcome the company."

"What do you mean you used to be alone?"

"Oh...um..." He worked up the courage to open his eyes, one at a time.

Jeddie, apparently sensing his unwillingness to answer the question, quickly said, "You know what, never mind. We agreed that you didn't have to answer questions today."

Peter wondered if his relief showed on his face. He relaxed, his grip on the railing lightening, and a smile appeared in the corner of his lips.

The two of them sat at the top of the tree until Kent walked out the back door and started down the pebble pathway. Peter knew then that it would soon be time to find his way down. However, just barely getting used to being at the top, he wasn't sure how he was going to do that.

Never before had he felt so calm while being so high up. He wasn't sure if that was due in part to the calming nature of all of the plants, or because of his new friend, Jeddie. He decided both were to thank.

"Thank you, for showing me this place," he said.

"You're welcome."

With caution, Peter took each step down with a firm grip on the stair railing. He was glad to have made it down to the yard just as Kent stepped through the back gate. It was embarrassing enough with Jeddie watching him; he didn't want Kent to see how afraid of heights he was.

"Okay," Kent said, "I thought I'd grill some burgers tonight. That sound good?"

"Perfect." They nodded in unison.

Jeddie set the table on the back patio while Kent grilled the burgers. "So, what do you think of the nursery, Peter?" Kent asked.

"It's pretty amazing."

"I'm glad you like it. Maybe since you and Jeddie are

partners for this term's project, you can come hang out here after school? I could even get you a job if you're looking to make a little extra money."

"I should talk to Elaine first," he said, clamming up.

The sun glimmered as the tree leaves blew from a soft breeze. Peter enjoyed the serenity of their yard. At Elaine's, the yard was overgrown and, with years of neglect, was wilted and bleak. He knew a yard took well-thought-out plans and meticulous care, and it made him feel relaxed finally being in one that didn't look like an impossible project.

With hands in his pocket, Peter stood at the edge of the patio. "How do you design a yard like this?"

"Well, it took a lot of work. And you're seeing the finished project after years of planting and tearing out and replanting. I had to be patient with myself as I learned which plants would thrive in our yard and which wouldn't." Kent stepped away from the grill and joined Peter. "I think the hard work has paid off."

"I'd say so."

"So, Peter, tell me about yourself," Kent said.

To Peter's relief, Jeddie chimed in. "No. Not today, Dad. Peter requested that today not be about him."

"Oh?" Kent questioned. "Well then, let's make it about you, Jeddie. I can tell him all about you," he said with a laugh.

"Yes...but you'll leave out anything embarrassing." Jeddie eyed him.

"Hey now. This is a 'get to know you' project. If you really want Peter to get to know you, then how can you leave out all the good stuff?"

"What do you want to know?" Jeddie asked, turning to Peter.

"I guess let's start with family. It's just the two of you?" Peter jumped in.

"Yep," she said resolutely. "My mom's out there some-where, but she and my dad split when I was a baby. I also had a brother that died when I was little."

"I'm so sorry."

"It's okay. I never met him." She shot a glance at her dad.

"Do you see your mom very often?"

"Never."

"Never?"

"That's right. Maybe you can answer that, Dad." She flipped her head back to him.

Kent cleared his throat. He seemed like he'd known this question was coming. "Well," he contemplated, "Jeddie's mom and I decided a long time ago that it was best if Jeddie just stay with me. I haven't seen her mom in a long time."

"Which means not only have I not seen her, but I've never even met her."

Peter could tell he'd touched a nerve and he looked down at his plate, embarrassed.

"And not only that," Jeddie decided to add, "I don't even know her name or what she looks like. The man won't show me a picture of her."

"Okay, Jeddie." Kent made a placating gesture. "You are making our guest uncomfortable."

The fire that Peter had unintentionally lit inside Jeddie quickly extinguished. "He's right. I'm sorry, Peter. It's just a bit of a rough subject around here."

Peter, Kent, and Jeddie sat at the table and started assembling their burgers. They made small talk about the nursery and their yard. As the sun started to set, Jeddie turned the patio lighting on so they wouldn't be stuck in the dark. After consuming most of their dinner, Peter wanted to make Jeddie feel less awkward about never seeing her mom.

"If it makes you feel any better, Jeddie, my dad died when I was just a baby. So maybe it's good that you at least know your mom is out there somewhere?"

"I don't know, sometimes I think it would be better if she were dead." She was so matter of fact that it startled Peter.

"Oookay!" Kent got up from the table. "I think that's enough for tonight. Ride home, Peter?"

"Uh, yep," Peter replied. He didn't dare say another word.

Kent eyed Jeddie as he went in the house. He returned a moment later with his car keys. "Alrighty, let's go."

Jeddie began clearing the table as they headed to the driveway.

The ride to Elaine's was quiet, neither of them knowing quite what to say. Jeddie and Kent's argument changed the mood of the night in a second, and Peter felt caught in the middle. As the car slowed in front of Elaine's house, the warm living room lights invited Peter in.

He didn't hesitate to open the car door. "Thanks for the ride, Mr. Sams." The formality felt appropriate.

"You bet, Peter. Have a good night."

"Unbelievable," Kent breathed out as he drove home quicker than usual, already preparing for the inevitable argument. When Kent shut the garage door behind him and walked into the kitchen, Jeddie was careful not to turn around.

"How many times am I going to have to explain it to you, Jed? How many times before you understand?" He paused for a response, but since she didn't give one, he continued. "I know you're upset that your mom isn't around, but you have to believe me that it's for the best. At the very least, could you stop with the attitude? It's getting old."

Jeddie kept her eyes on the bowl she was washing. Kent watched as she tried to subtly move her hair to shield her face, but it was too late; Kent had seen the tears.

"Look," Kent said gently, approaching and putting a hand on her shoulder. "I'm sorry."

Jeddie let her tears fall freely as she started to sob.

Kent continued. "It was a decision I made a long time ago. And maybe it wasn't the right decision, but I have to believe it is."

With soapy, wet hands, Jeddie turned and cried into his shoulder.

"Please be patient with me, Jed. I'm trying my best."

"I know."

He pulled her head away from his shoulder and looked into her eyes. He gently kissed her forehead and whispered, "I love you, sweetie. Never forget that." He let her hug him again, and his heart broke, knowing she was hurting. "You go wash up, okay? I can finish here."

Jeddie headed out of the kitchen and upstairs to her bathroom. When Kent heard her close the door, he placed his palms on the counter in front of him and started to sob.

WHEN FRIDAY CAME AROUND, the whole school was buzzing with excitement over the upcoming baseball game that afternoon. Students wore school colors, and banners announcing the game hung in every hallway. Teachers were more relaxed and gave minimal assignments so students could attend the game.

It seemed as if the whole town had gathered for the game. The bleachers were filling up and lawn chairs and shade umbrellas popped up sporadically over the field. Peter had asked Elaine earlier in the week if she would attend with him. Although he and Jeddie had become friends, he wasn't quite ready to be immersed in a circle of her girlfriends. He and Elaine found seats on the bleachers, and Peter knew that having Elaine there would get him through this new experience.

The crowd was bustling with excitement, watching the team warm-up. Jeddie sat with her friend on a blanket on the lawn. Natalie eyed Peter when he passed with Elaine.

"So that's Peter," she said, leaning in close to Jeddie.

"That's Peter."

"He's really cute."

"You're not wrong." Jeddie smiled.

"Come on. You got to give me something."

"There's nothing to give. I don't know much about him."

"You spent the afternoon together."

"I know, but he insisted that the focus be on me. He didn't want to talk about himself."

"Mysterious," Natalie joked.

Just then, Kent came up behind the girls. "How are my girls doing?"

"We're good, Dad."

"Good to hear. Well, I better go find a seat on the bleachers."

"Peter just got here. Maybe you could sit by him." Jeddie pointed to where he was sitting.

"Great, thanks," he said, walking away. When he made it

to the bleachers, he approached Peter and said, "Do you mind if I sit here?"

"No, not at all." He and Elaine scooted to make room.

Elaine leaned over Peter to see who had joined them. "Kent Sams?"

He looked over at her. "Oh my! Professor Watts? I can't believe it's you!"

"What has it been, ten years?"

"More like fifteen."

"I can't believe that. What have you been up to?"

Peter chimed in. "How do you two know each other?"

"Kent was my student," Elaine explained.

"Really?"

"Yep. Back in my prime," Kent laughed.

"How do you two know each other?" Elaine asked, gesturing between Kent and Peter.

"This is Jeddie's dad," Peter said.

"The famous Jeddie I keep hearing about? You'll have to invite her over sometime so I can get to know her."

"I'm sure she'd really like that," Kent said.

Dalesprings threw the first pitch and the game was off. Peter was mesmerized. Elaine and Kent kept talking and catching up, but Peter might as well have been sitting alone on the bleachers, he was so captivated by the game. He had only ever seen a baseball game on TV, and to be there in person felt surreal. As the crowd roared when the first player came across home plate, he put his hand in his pocket and clasped it around Lou. Tonight, he felt like he was with his dad.

## 5

While Elaine puttered around the kitchen the next morning, Peter stood at the sliding glass door staring out at her backyard. It looked like an untamed jungle. He thought back to Kent's pristine yard.

"What's on your mind, kiddo?" Elaine asked.

Pulled out of his thoughts, Peter turned to Elaine. "I was just looking at the yard."

"I know. It's a mess."

"I was just wondering...Why did you stop?"

"Stop what?"

"Well, you were a horticulture professor. I guess I was just surprised to hear that."

She stood beside him with her hands on her hips, surveying the backyard. "I don't know. At first, my attention was devoted to Larry. Now...I look at that mess and don't even know where to start."

"Maybe I could help...or maybe Kent could?"

"No. I could never live with myself if one of my students saw this place."

"Elaine..."

"Do you know how often I gave them lectures on maintaining their yards?"

"He would understand."

Elaine still looked ashamed of herself, but nodded. "I'll think about it."

~

A FEW DAYS LATER, Jeddie and Peter rode their bikes to Ted's —a local diner and gathering place for all ages. Jeddie was still embarrassed about fighting with Kent in front of Peter. If she was honest with herself, she hadn't realized how much pent-up emotion she had on the subject of her mom. Not wanting to embarrass herself anymore, she was determined to keep the focus on Peter today.

Ted's Diner had become one of Jeddie's favorite places. She and Kent had started a tradition a few years back to come to the diner once a month. They easily spent a lot of time together running the nursery, but never had a chance for daddy-daughter time. For both of them, a night away from the nursery once a month was just enough to rejuvenate.

When they walked inside, the aroma of fried chicken engulfed them. Jeddie pointed to the swivel stools at the counter—her favorite place to sit. There she could talk with the owner, Ted. When the waitress came, Jeddie ordered two chocolate milkshakes and a plate of fries to share before they pulled their schoolwork out of their backpacks. Mr. Jensen had provided each student with a list of suggested questions to help them get started on their project.

Jeddie eyed the page of questions. It made her feel silly. All of the questions were generic: *What is your favorite food? When were you born? What is your favorite color?* She reasoned that if she really wanted to get to know Peter, the scripted questions would have to go. She stuffed them back in her backpack and drummed her thumbs on the counter. Peter was still staring at his page.

"Peter?"

"Yeah?"

"I think we should just put these away." She slipped the paper out of his hand and placed it face-down on the counter. "I think we can do better than the questions on this page." She eyed him, hoping he would be more comfortable telling his story now that he'd seen her embarrass herself.

"Okay," Peter said warily.

"I realize we don't know each other all that well, but I can tell you are really nervous about this project."

Peter stared at his hands.

"Come on, Peter. You can trust me." She rested her forearms on the table and leaned closer to him.

"All right. But anything I tell you...I don't want you telling anyone else."

"Of course."

"I mean it."

He was so serious that it startled Jeddie. "Okay. But, Peter, I'm going to need to share something about you for the project."

"I know. Just not what I tell you today. Okay?"

"Okay." She didn't know what to expect, and wasn't sure now if she wanted to know what he was going to tell her.

Muffled voices of other customers filled the diner. Fried food scented the air. She watched him as he formulated his thoughts. The first few times he went to speak, he opened his mouth and nothing came out; he would simply close it again, still holding back. Jeddie almost stepped in to tell him he didn't have to tell her, when he finally began.

"I told the class that I live with my aunt, but that isn't true. Elaine isn't my aunt. She's my foster mom."

Jeddie processed in silence. She adjusted her position in the seat and leaned against the back of the chair to get a better look at him.

"I was taken from my mom a couple of months ago."

"Oh," was all Jeddie could muster.

"That was the worst day," Peter said, before adding, "But also the best day."

"What do you mean?"

Disregarding her question, he asked, "Is it terrible that I don't miss her?"

Jeddie didn't answer.

"I've tried to figure it out. I mean, who reported my mom? Someone must have. But who? Because I can only think of a handful of people that knew I lived there."

"Lived where?"

Right then, the waitress came with their order. "Two chocolate milkshakes, and a plate of fries," she said with a smile. "Can I get y'all anything else?"

Jeddie, still processing what Peter had told her, just smiled at the waitress. It was Peter that jumped in, saying, "I think this is good, thanks."

After the waitress left, silence descended. Jeddie pulled a fry from the plate, happy to occupy her mouth. Peter slowly slurped his milkshake.

Jeddie finally broke their silence. "I'm sorry, Peter. I can't even imagine." After replaying Peter's words in her mind, she asked, "What did you mean about only a few people knowing where you lived?"

He took smalls sips of his milkshake, looking deep in thought and as worried as ever, like he was struggling to find the right words to tell her something he'd rather not.

The pair looked at each other. Jeddie remained patient, trying to radiate understanding and empathy without being too intense.

"This is what I've been dreading telling you. I don't really know how to tell anyone about where I grew up."

At this point, Jeddie half-expected him to tell her that he was the real-life Tarzan, raised in the jungle by gorillas.

"I grew up at Lakewood Residence Center. Have you heard of it?"

She shook her head.

"It's a residence facility that takes care of those who are mentally disabled."

Her attention became acute.

"When I was eight, we lost our home—my mom and me."

Jeddie's mouth slipped open, but before she could say anything, Peter continued.

"My mom works at Lakewood, and with their permission, they leased one of the rooms to my mom so we could have a place to live. I thought we would only be there for a short time while my mom figured out what to do, but we never left. Lakewood became our home."

Jeddie noted how intensely Peter was looking at her, as if he was trying to read her mind. Peter winced, and Jeddie hoped he wasn't taking her silence as some kind of judgment. She tried to keep her tone and expression even, but wasn't sure she was succeeding as she processed what Peter had just told her. She was trying to picture Lakewood, but it seemed like such an odd situation. Now knowing where he grew up, it started to make more sense why he was so hesitant about this project. She suddenly felt guilty for complaining about not knowing her mom. From what she could tell, Peter had a much harder childhood than she'd had.

"So, you've never been able to get back in your house?" she asked.

"Nope."

"And because of that, you lived at your mom's work, which just so happens to be a mental facility?"

"Uh, yep."

"So, you grew up in a mental facility."

He nodded.

"Huh." Jeddie gulped her shake while dipping her fries in ketchup. "Were you close to any of the patients?"

"Yeah. Some of them. One of my friends, Kenny, he has Down syndrome; he always knew how to bring a smile to my face."

Jeddie thought back to seeing Peter with Marcus at lunch. It started to make sense why they had been instant friends. *Peter must be one of the most kind-hearted people I've ever met*, Jeddie thought.

Her mind was processing so fast she could hardly keep up with her thoughts. "What happened to your house? Was it repossessed by the bank?"

"I have no idea."

"What do you mean?"

"I mean I have no idea. I've tried to get my mom to tell me how we lost our house, but she's really secretive about it. And I've never been back to that house. My mom refused to take me."

"For real?"

"Yeah. When I was younger, and we had just started living at Lakewood, I would ask her all the time. She brushed it off lightly at first, but as I got older, and really started to pester her about it, she got upset. She got so mad one time that she threw a plate at the wall." Peter snapped his mouth shut, seemingly worried he'd said too much.

Jeddie's eyes widened. "Did she hit you?"

"Oh no. She would never do that."

Jeddie was skeptical. "Peter, she threw a plate at the wall. That's not normal. Are you sure she never did anything violent to you?"

"I'm sure. I shouldn't have told you that. Please, don't make a big deal out of it."

Jeddie was upset about it though, and felt it was a bigger deal than Peter was letting on, but she worried if she didn't let it go then Peter would close up.

She decided to change the subject. "So, tell me what you remember about your house."

His eyes lit up as he began describing his house. Just like at the nursery, Jeddie saw the tension in his shoulders ease. It was like a different side of Peter—a part of him coming back to life.

"Okay, I hope you don't think I'm weird for carrying this in my pocket, but this is the one thing I have from my house." He reached into his pocket and pulled out a small Lego character that he placed on the counter. "I've kept him in my pocket every day we lived at Lakewood. I don't think my mom even knew I had it. I was afraid that, if she knew, she would have taken him from me."

The comment rattled Jeddie again, but she tried to hide her frustration.

"When I was little," Peter continued, "I loved Legos. Everything about them. I got a little obsessed one year and built a house in my room. A house that I could fit in."

"Really?"

"I know. A bit weird, but I loved it." He was quick to add, "Remember, I was eight."

"No, I think it's cool."

"Okay, well, I called it my castle. And I had all these toy figurines. I had some of them live at the castle and others that would try to destroy it. I would play all the time with these figurines, and Lou here was my favorite." He picked the Lego character off the counter.

"Lou?"

"Yeah, that's what I named him."

Jeddie held out her hand so she could get a closer look.

He retracted his hand at first, seemingly out of habitual instinct, but quickly handed him over.

"Why 'Lou'?" Jeddie asked.

"I named him in honor of my dad. Lou Gehrig is a baseball legend that died of a disease called ALS, which is what my dad had."

Jeddie turned the Lego over in her hand. She was overwhelmed by everything Peter had told her. And on top of everything, he had grown up in a mental facility.

"Peter...I don't know what to say."

"It's okay. You just listening has been enough," Peter said. Jeddie could almost see the weight that had been lifted from his shoulders. He seemed happy to have someone share the burden of his secrets.

Jeddie was happy to listen, even though having no response made her feel foolish. She wanted to do something more for him. She stared down at Lou, still in her hand, then stood him up by their plate of fries. While she slurped the last of her milkshake, she had an idea for what might just be the perfect thing she could do for Peter.

## 6

The next morning, Peter stumbled his way to the bathroom through partially closed eyes. He looked in the mirror and saw that his hair was matted on one side and stuck up on the other. With a yawn, he rubbed his eyes and decided he couldn't be bothered to do his hair. His mom wasn't there to rag on him about it, so he welcomed the opportunity to leave it.

He felt like he was still dreaming as he contemplated the previous afternoon. Even though Jeddie had been understanding, his mind jumped to his secret spreading through the whole school.

His feet clunked down each stair as he made his way to the kitchen where Elaine greeted him. "Well, good morning, Sleepy Head."

"Hello," he said through a yawn. He stood at the open refrigerator, gazing at its contents. He wasn't deciding what he should eat so much as distracting himself from the things on his mind.

"What sounds good to you? You want me to whip something up?" Elaine asked.

"I don't know." Peter shrugged.

Elaine looked concerned. "You okay, kiddo? You were pretty quiet about your outing with Jeddie yesterday."

"How do you do that?"

"Do what?"

"Know something was wrong. You just seem to know me so well."

"I pay attention," she said, looking pleased with herself.

He shut the refrigerator and softly banged his head on the door. "Lakewood came up yesterday."

"Oh." She nodded her head as if everything made sense now. "How did Jeddie take it?"

"She was great." Peter finally turned to look at her. "She was almost too understanding."

"What makes you say that?"

Peter relayed the conversation of the day before—how he'd told Jeddie about living at Lakewood, being in foster care, his dad dying.

"Wow, you two talked a lot."

"What do I do if she starts telling other kids at school?"

"Do you think she will?"

"I don't know. I hope not." He tapped his fingers on the counter.

"Did you ask her not to?"

"Yeah, but—"

"Then you just have to believe she won't. If she is anything like her dad, you don't have anything to worry about."

"How do you know?"

"Just a gut feeling." She got up from her barstool and limped over to make breakfast, her knee evidently acting up.

He took her spot at the counter, quickly becoming lost in thought.

Elaine must have sensed his unease, as she surprised him by saying, "Okay, you eat, and we will get you to school in time for your second period." Peter wasn't sure why he was surprised; Elaine always seemed very in tune with his moods and worries. When she made light of him missing his first class, he was extremely grateful for the extra time to regroup and process his thoughts.

With books in her arms, Jeddie stood on her toes and peered over the crowd to spot Peter. She thought Peter's locker would be the best place to meet him before heading to their first class with Mr. Jensen.

She was anxious to see him again after their conversation yesterday. Her thoughts about Peter and everything they'd talked about had kept her awake all night.

When the five-minute warning bell rang and Peter still hadn't showed, she started to worry. At the one-minute warning, she gave up her resolve and headed to class, almost not making it to her seat by the time the tardy bell rang.

"Good morning, class."

"Good morning, Mr. Jensen."

The morning formality always broke the ice and let the students know Mr. Jensen expected their attention.

"How are your projects going? It's been about a week, anyone want to share what they have been doing?"

Jeddie squirmed.

"Yes, Karen."

Karen shot up straight in her chair. "Tyler took me long-boarding yesterday. It was really fun to experience his favorite hobby." Karen knew Jeddie had a crush on Tyler, and she glanced over in her direction to smirk at her.

"That's great. And you were both wearing a helmet, I presume?"

"Yes."

"So, what made you want to share your hobby, Tyler?"

"That list of questions you gave us. It was super helpful to get started."

*Of course it was,* Jeddie retorted in her mind. *If only I would have kept to the questions.*

She glanced at the door, hoping Peter would walk through any minute. His absence was making her more uncomfortable with every passing minute.

"Perfect. That is exactly what those questions are for—a guideline to get you started."

Jeddie decided to pull the questions out of her bag and mull them over.

"All right, with that said, I am giving you the rest of the period to work with your partner. If you haven't started on your project, now would be the time." He eyed the students. "Start with these questions, and then move on to something more."

Mr. Jensen excused the class to get to work, and the students rearranged desks to pair up.

"Oh, Jeddie," Mr. Jensen called for her attention. "Peter's aunt called in and he won't be able to make it to class today. Maybe you could join another partnership for today."

"That's okay. I have plenty to work on." *The last thing I want is to have small talk with another group.*

He gave her a thumbs up.

Karen looked at her friends and mimicked Jeddie. "That's okay," she mouthed mockingly. Her friends laughed.

Jeddie ignored her and began to look over the questions.

She came to the same conclusion she had yesterday; the questions were lame. *What is your favorite color? What do you want to be when you grow up? What is your favorite food?* The questions were surface-level. There was no way she would have learned what she did about Peter yesterday if she had just asked these questions.

But then again, Peter was absent today, and she worried it was due to her going off script yesterday.

It was a lot for her to process, and she was only seeing the situation from the outside. She couldn't imagine actually living through what Peter had. *Growing up in a mental hospital? That had to be odd.*

She took a pen out from her bag and scribbled down one word. *Lakewood.* Jeddie may have promised she would keep Lakewood a secret, but she didn't promise that she would stay away from there.

With renewed determination, she firmly underlined the word and decided she was going to find out what Lakewood was all about. If she really wanted to get to know Peter, she would just have to see for herself where he grew up. All that was left to do was devise a plan.

"HEY. HOW'S IT GOING?" Peter asked as Jeddie approached his locker.

She had been looking at her phone, texting Peter. "Hey. Everything okay?" She stuffed her phone in her back pocket.

"Yep. You?"

She ignored his question. "Were you sick this morning?"

"Oh. No. I just had a slow start."

"Okay." She wanted him to expound, but didn't want to push. "Glad you're here now."

She eyed him as he shuffled through the contents of his locker. *Did that slow start have anything to do with yesterday?* she thought. She tried to read what he was feeling, but he seemed fine, as if yesterday was any ordinary day. She resolved that if he was going to act normal, there was no reason for her not to.

"Hey, Peter?"

"Yeah?"

"Do you think you would be able to find your house if we tried?"

"My house?"

"Yeah, the house you lived in when you were little. I just thought that maybe it would be fun to go see it now. Maybe meet the family that owns it. See what it looks like. Tell them that you used to live there. What do you think?"

He hid his face behind the door of his locker. "Oh. I'm not sure. Don't you think that would be a little weird? Just showing up like that?"

"Maybe, but I bet the owner wouldn't mind."

It's not that he wasn't curious. Going back to his old house was something he had always wanted, but now that he was out of Lakewood, he wondered if it was a good idea to go poking around the past.

Regardless, he found himself agreeing with Jeddie. "I guess we could try. It's been a long time, but I bet if we rode around, I would start to recognize landmarks."

"Really?"

Peter nodded. "Yeah, we could do that."

Jeddie was so excited that her grin stretched across her whole face. Digging in the past was something she loved to do. She had been expecting Peter to say he didn't want to go. Now that he agreed, she couldn't wait to get going.

MOUNTAIN VIEW BORDERED the west side of Dalesprings. Mountain View was smaller in size, but comparative in population. About thirty minutes into their bike ride, they started to glide into the center of town.

As they pulled onto the main road, Jeddie's eyes lit up. "Wow, that's so beautiful."

Vibrant red and yellow tulips bloomed in the median between road lanes. The clean lines of each color made Jeddie's heart jump. In the center of the shops, a roundabout was circled with deep purple tulips. She felt like she was in the Netherlands; she had never seen so many tulips in one place.

"Peter, isn't this amazing?" Jeddie yelled over her shoulder before realizing Peter had stopped following her. "Peter?"

She pulled off to the sidewalk and turned her head, spotting him walking through the door of an ice cream shop, disappearing inside.

*That's weird. Why is he going in there?*

She pushed her right foot against the concrete to get momentum going and turned the bike around to meet up with him.

She entered the shop and looked around. There were tall tables in the back, short tables in the front. Up at the counter, there was a vast display of ice cream buckets. She watched as Peter eyed them all, his gaze finally settling on Mint Fudge Chunk.

Behind him, Jeddie spoke. "You know this place?"

Peter jumped, appearing startled by her voice. "Yeah, my mom used to bring me here. The owner, Marty, became a good friend of ours."

The boy at the register told Peter that he would be right with them as he finished helping another customer. Peter smiled and nodded at him.

"How old were you?" Jeddie asked.

"Close to eight. We would come here about once a week before..." Peter replied before trailing off, warily eyeing the other customers in the shop.

Jeddie gave him a sympathetic look, not knowing what to say. She was grateful when their awkward moment was interrupted.

"Sorry about the wait. What can I get for you two?"

Before ordering, Peter asked, "Is Marty around?"

"No," the boy answered, "Marty passed away a couple of years ago. I'm his grandson, Colin."

"Oh. I'm so sorry," Peter said.

"How did you know him?"

"I used to come here with my mom when I was little."

"I bet he loved that. My grandpa always loved being around kids."

"I'm very sorry."

"Thank you. We sure miss him," Colin replied. "Can I get you a scoop on the house?"

"I couldn't let you do that." Peter waved his hand.

"Really, I insist."

With a little more hassling, Colin convinced both Peter and Jeddie to choose which ice cream they each wanted. Peter thanked him over and over as they walked to the bench outside the shop.

"I'm sorry about Marty," Jeddie said as they sat down.

"It's okay. I'm honestly just happy to see that his family has kept his shop running. It's one of the best places in town. Marty's grandson is great. Just like Marty."

"Yeah, Colin was really nice," Jeddie said, smiling to

herself. She had begun to question if there were any positive moments from Peter's childhood, and seeing him at the ice cream shop put those thoughts at ease.

"I'm really glad we came here," Peter said.

"I'm glad we did too. Did your mom take you anywhere else?" She was hopeful that by remembering the ice cream shop, he would know how to make his way to his house.

"No, not really. She was always busy working, so it was nice just to have this place."

She looked at Peter as he shoved the last bite of his cone in his mouth, too anxious to keep sitting at the ice cream shop all day. "So, do you think you could find your house from here?"

He choked a little and put his hand to his mouth to keep his cone from coming out. "Um, yeah, actually. It's a little ways out, but I think I could get us there."

"Perfect. Let's go." She sprang up from the bench and perched on her bike, waiting for Peter to join.

THEY STARTED on their bikes headed out of town and into the suburbs of Mountain View. After circling streets for thirty minutes, Peter could tell that Jeddie was starting to give up hope.

"Is anything looking familiar?" she asked.

Peter's head swayed from side to side as he looked at the houses and street names. He shook his head. "Nothing on this street."

They had slowed down so much that Jeddie was having trouble balancing on her bike. She gave up and planted both feet on the asphalt. "I'm sorry, Peter. I thought this would be a good idea."

Now more determined than ever to find his house, he suggested, "Maybe if we went back to the park one more time? I might be able to find it from there."

One last time, they went back to the park and chose a different route. Peter's chest started to tighten when he recognized a street sign. "I think this is it." He began to pedal faster. The neighborhoods started to look more familiar as they drew closer to his house. "I had a friend who lived in this house." He pointed to the right as they passed a red-bricked home.

"This is it!" Peter pointed ahead. "The next street." Excited, Peter pedaled harder, raising up off the seat. When he turned the corner, his home came into view and he sank back onto the seat, overcome with shock. His feet stopped moving, no longer able to pedal.

The momentum of the wheels was the only thing pushing him forward. He was so shocked by what he saw that his bike barely made it to the front of his house before it crawled to a stop. Jeddie rounded the corner and saw what Peter was looking at.

"Oh, Peter," she said sympathetically.

In a swift, dazed movement, Peter stepped off his bike, his mouth gaped open. With his eyes fixed on the door, he set his bike on the sidewalk and strode across the front yard. Jeddie stepped off her bike, standing still on the curb as Peter trudged to the door.

He looked from one end of the house to the other. The windows were boarded up with wood that had become rotted, the once-white side paneling was black from ash and soot, and the roof had caved in over the garage.

Peter made it to the door and hesitated with his hand on the handle. When he gave it a twist, he was surprised that the door creaked open. The pressure of the door opening rustled dried leaves on the wooden floor inside. The stairs in the entryway had collapsed, the railing protruded into the hallway. The small chandelier that had once hung from the ceiling lay shattered across the floor. The sun shining in from the window caused reflected prisms to dance on the wall. He took a step inside and looked into the living room. The neatly decorated and cozy room he remembered was now piled with broken and dilapidated furniture.

Peter could hear Jeddie's approaching footsteps, but they stopped before she reached the porch. He held back tears, knowing she was right behind him. He was in so much shock that he was pulled into a trance, scanning the entryway until his curiosity nudged him into the house. He couldn't help but want to see the rest of the home he had loved. He wanted to look everywhere, but one room drew him in more than any other. He ducked underneath the railing, slumped over, and began inching his way down the hall as shards of glass crunched under his shoes. When he was able to stand upright again, it was only a few steps more until he made it to his bedroom.

The door was already open a crack and he gave it a gentle press to get a better look inside. He was so taken aback he could hardly breathe. Though everything was mostly intact, in the corner of his room, he saw his Lego house he had been so proud of. Bricks of all colors had melted together from the heat of the fire. He ran to the house, his hand shaking as he touched the drooping brick where the roof had caved in. No longer able to control his tears, he dropped to his knees and started to cry when he saw all of his old figurines, some of them totally disfigured.

It was as if he was eight again. "I'm so sorry," he sobbed. "I should have protected you." He picked up several toys and held them in his arms. "I should have never left. How did this happen?" He held a soldier and examined him. He was missing an arm, and his face sagged on one side. "I'm so sorry, colonel. I didn't mean for this to happen." He pulled the soldier close, hugging him as his tears landed on the dry floor. His chest became tight. *Why didn't my mom ever tell me our house burned down?*

He held onto his soldier for a long time. The sun hit Peter's face, and as he composed himself, his tears became sticky on his cheeks. He ran his finger along the door of his Lego house and reflected on the hours and days it had taken him to build and design a house he could fit inside of. But now all he could see were the demolished remains of a kingdom he had once been so proud of. Loving memories of his childhood forever replaced by the fire that took them away.

He let warm tears pool in his tired eyes and run down his cheeks, sniffling to keep his nose from running.

Consumed by his bedroom, he had completely forgotten Jeddie was there until he felt a hand on his shoulder.

"I'm so sorry, Peter."

He pulled his shoulder from her in anger. "Why did you make me come here? I would have never seen my house like this if you had just left it alone."

"Peter, I..." She stared at him, seemingly trying to string her words together.

"Just leave me alone."

"Peter?" Her eyes widened.

"Get out of here."

"I didn't mean...I didn't know...I'm sorry." The last words came out as a whisper.

"Get out of here, Jeddie!" he said, definitely not in a whisper.

TEARS WELLED in Jeddie's eyes as she curtly turned on her heel, making her exit. On her hands and knees, she crawled under the banister. She had forgotten about the broken chandelier and let out a yelp of pain when she felt a shard of glass scathe her knee.

She followed Peter's command and started on her bike ride home. The tears in her eyes made all the streets blurry, but she pedaled faster until she saw the park they had passed on their way into the neighborhood. Unable to control her emotions, she pulled over when she saw a bench. She walked around and around it before finally slumping down onto it and letting the tears fall down her cheeks. Thoughts flooded her mind. *How could Peter blame me? There is no way I could have known.* She inhaled and exhaled deeply in an attempt to control her heart rate. *This is not my fault, right?* She went back and forth from being completely mad at Peter for his reaction, to agreeing with him that it was her fault for going there in the first place.

Looking at the steady trickle of blood down her leg, she figured there was nothing she could do to fix the situation or her knee by just sitting there. She got back on her bike and headed home to Dalesprings.

When she pulled into her garage, she looked at her watch and was glad it was early enough that Kent would still be at the nursery. She headed straight for the bathroom, determined to wash the horrible day off of her. Turning the water temperature as hot as she could stand, she let the steam fill the room. She hoped the hot water would help disguise her red, swollen eyes before her dad came home and started asking about her day.

PETER, still curled up on the floor, didn't realize how long he had been in his old bedroom until the moonlight shone through the window. Thinking about how worried Elaine must be, he shuffled to his feet. On his way to the door, he knocked into the dresser and heard a crunch under his foot. Grateful he had shoes on, he looked to see a fallen old picture frame spread across the floor. He picked it up gingerly, spilling the broken glass onto the floor before taking the picture out to examine it. The picture was taken just weeks before he and his mom went to Lakewood.

His mom had taken him to the zoo for his birthday, and the two of them were standing in front of the gorilla cage—Peter's favorite. He looked into his mom's eyes. She seemed so happy. Peter couldn't remember the last time he saw his mom smile the way she had in the picture. For the first time since he'd been taken from her, he missed her—not the person she was at Lakewood, but the person she was in this picture. His lips quirked upward in a small, closed-mouth smile as he folded the picture to fit into his pocket.

The bike ride to Elaine's was quiet except for the occasional cars whooshing by. Peter's head swam with thoughts as he tried to piece his life story together. He still couldn't understand why his mom didn't just tell him their house had burned down.

The bike ride was all too short. Before he knew it, he was on Elaine's street. With a puff of his cheeks, he blew his hair out of his face. The living room light was on, which meant Elaine was waiting for him. Unable to avoid her, he took a deep breath in and pushed the door open, knowing that with the tears on his face and his swollen eyes, he would have no choice but to tell her what had happened.

## 7

After her long shower, Jeddie paced her bedroom floor, music blasted from her headphones. Images of Peter's house flashed in her mind—the boarded-up windows, the pile of charred furniture, the staircase and shattered chandelier. She looked down at her knee, now bandaged up. *How could he blame me for this? There was no way I could have known.*

Shaking her head, she decided to lie flat on her back on the soft white rug in the middle of her room, closing her eyes. She rapidly went through a range of emotions, feeling her face alternate between flushing red with anger and draining with guilt. Ultimately, she was disappointed that a day she had anticipated being a cool experience for Peter ended up being a huge disaster.

When Kent's sock-covered foot nudged her arm, she opened one eye. She could see his silhouette outlined against the ceiling light, and caught the end of his sentence as she pulled her headphones out of her ears.

"...want for dinner?" His voice was raised.

She sat up, crossing her legs. "I don't know."

"I think we should get out tonight. Wanna go into town?"

Going into town was the last thing Jeddie wanted. "I was hoping we could stay in tonight."

"Uh, sure. Sure." Kent nodded and clapped his hands together. "I'll, uh, go get started."

"Great, I'll be right down."

KENT LAID out an array of food on the counter. Tonight would be a concoction of whatever they had in the fridge.

Jeddie came in the kitchen and Kent gave her a big smile.

"All right, Miss Let's Cook At Home, here's our spread tonight. We have eggs, peppers, ham, and tomatoes, so I'm thinking...omelets. How's that sound?"

"Perfect."

Jeddie stood silent at the counter, cutting the peppers. At the stove, Kent was wondering how to break the ice. The last time he had come home to Jeddie laying in the middle of the floor blasting her music, it took her a week to come out of her bad mood.

He decided to jump right in. "So, how was your day? You and Peter were together this afternoon, right?"

"Uh, yeah."

Kent continued to pry. "What did you do?"

"Just hung out."

He had a feeling it was going to be a long night of him asking questions and Jeddie giving short answers. He had always tried his best, but communicating with a teenage daughter when she was upset was not his forte. He stopped whipping the eggs and turned around.

"Come on, Jeddie Bear." He put his hands on her shoulders. "What's up? What happened today to make you upset?"

Jeddie's shoulders shrugged underneath his hands. He could tell she was trying to hold it in, but a tear ran down her cheek and dripped onto the counter.

"Did Peter do something?"

"No," she spat, before quickly admitting, "Maybe."

He wondered if he wanted to know what a teenage boy did to make his daughter upset, but he knew it was necessary to find out. "What did he do?"

Jeddie turned to face Kent, but her head was still pointed toward the floor.

"I thought it would be a good idea to go to Peter's old hometown today. I don't know...I thought maybe if I got him back in his childhood element, he would open up a bit more..." She looked up at Kent. "It was a mistake."

"You've got to give me more than that. What happened?"

Jeddie rolled her eyes, but Kent got the sense it was directed more at herself than at him. She walked around the counter and sat at the table while Kent finished cooking and served up their plates.

"It started out really good. We biked through the middle of town, and Peter recognized this ice cream shop he and his mom used to go to."

Kent carried their food to the table and joined her.

"We talked to the owner's grandson and he gave us ice cream on the house. It was cool, and Peter seemed so happy to have reconnected with part of his childhood." Jeddie paused before adding, "Then we went to see the home where he grew up."

"Not good?"

"No, not good."

Kent inched forward, waiting for an explanation.

"Dad, his house had burned down."

Kent, not expecting that scenario, sunk back into his chair. "It burned down?"

"It was boarded up and part of the roof was caved in. It was awful...Peter went inside, and he was in there for so long that I ended up following him." She took a bite of eggs before continuing. "I was surprised when I went inside that his bedroom was in relatively good condition." She laughed to herself before adding, "He must have been some creative kid, because he had built this house out of Legos that filled a quarter of his room. It was really cool, except that the Legos had melted from the heat of the fire and had partly collapsed in on itself."

"You went inside?"

She must have sensed Kent's disapproval as she replied, "I'm okay, Dad." She waited for him to relax and then continued. "When I went into the room, Peter was sobbing. I put my hand on his shoulder to try to show him how sorry I was. But he must have not cared or realized, because he just started yelling at me. He was mad about the house, and he was mad at me because it was my idea to go there."

"You couldn't have known, sweetie."

"I know, but Peter made me feel like it was all my fault."

"Did he say anything on your way home?"

"We didn't come home together."

"What do you mean you didn't come home together?"

She became defensive. "He kept yelling at me to leave. I didn't want to, but he just yelled louder. So, I ran out of there and biked home. For all I know, he could still be there."

"We need to call Elaine."

"Elaine? Why?"

"If he is still gone, she's going to be worried about him."

"I'm sure he's fine," Jeddie said, her anger clearly clouding her judgment.

"Jeddie. Call her."

With an annoyed look, Jeddie pulled out her phone. and scanned for Elaine's number. Peter had shared it with her just in case of an emergency. She dialed the number and handed the phone to Kent. "Here. You can talk to her."

JEDDIE HAD BEEN RIGHT ABOUT one thing that night: Peter was fine. When Kent spoke to Elaine, she had told him that Peter had come home upset and she couldn't console him. After her attempts to coax him into telling her what had happened, she sent him to his room. Kent relayed Jeddie's side of the story.

"Thank you, Kent. I'll call you in the morning after I hear more from Peter."

Kent hung up and gave the phone back to Jeddie. "I'm just glad he's okay. It sounds like both of you have some apologizing to do."

"Me?"

"Jeddie, you shouldn't have left him there. That was really irresponsible."

"You didn't see him yelling at me, Dad."

"I get that, but it wasn't good to leave him there alone."

Jeddie replayed Kent's words in her head that night, unable to fall asleep. The events of the afternoon kept rolling in her mind. She had been so angry with Peter, but her anger had faded when she'd tried putting herself in Peter's place, imagining how it would have been to see an old home burned down—all possessions ruined, memories tarnished. She felt remorseful and tried to come up with a way she could make the afternoon up to Peter. Without any ideas, her mind finally shut off and she was able to drift to sleep just as the morning sun was starting to rise.

.

## 8

In the cafeteria at Lakewood, Peter sat surrounded by the other residents, who had gathered for his twelfth birthday. He had gotten used to celebrating his birthdays at Lakewood and he had to admit that he liked spending his birthday with the friends he had made there, especially Kenny. Peter had always admired Kenny's ability to love others unconditionally. He always made Peter feel like he was the most important person in the world, like he really mattered. He didn't feel that way very often at Lakewood.

When Lisa brought out the cake, candles lit, Kenny jumped up and down, excited that Peter got to make a wish.

"Make it a good one!" Kenny said with a thumbs up.

Lisa leaned in close to Peter and whispered, "I just wish this coming year is as good as last year."

Peter thought that was an odd comment. He didn't wish that at all. In fact, he wished this coming year would bring something new...something outside of Lakewood.

He puffed his cheeks at the end of everyone's singing

and blew hard, hoping that when he opened his eyes, his wish would come true.

"PETER?" Angela asked.

Peter had dazed off in thought. "Yeah?"

"Is everything okay? I lost you for a minute."

"Yeah, I'm fine."

"You were about to tell me what happened last night. Elaine said it would be good for you to get it off your chest and talk to someone."

"It sounds like she already told you, so…"

Elaine gave Angela a wary glance. Peter had made so much progress over the last couple of months. To see it come to a halt because he saw his old home would be discouraging.

"Elaine is just worried, Peter. She cares about you."

"Well, maybe I would be better off if everyone just gave me some space." He got up and walked out of the room.

Angela and Elaine looked at each other.

"Maybe he's right, Angela. Maybe we do need to give him some time to process what happened last night."

Elaine knew how long Peter had dreamed about seeing his old home, and how disheartening it must have been to see it in the condition that it was. She figured he'd probably worked up his childhood to be an idealized fantasy compared to what was essentially his cage at Lakewood. For that fantasy to be lost in a fire…It was hard for Elaine to imagine what was going through Peter's head.

IT WASN'T unusual for Jeddie to wake up to an empty house and get herself off to school on days that Kent woke up early to get ahead of the nursery's business rush. However, due to the short amount of sleep she'd had the night before, she slept through her morning alarm.

A dream she had been having startled her enough that her right eye popped open. Her left eye, smashed against her pillow, stayed closed. Without moving, she looked around her bedroom. The morning light indicated that she had woken up late, but instead of being panicked like she usually would have been, she stayed still. She gazed at the crinkled paper that had missed her trashcan, piles of notes and books on her desk, the pile of dirty clothes on the floor.

*I need to do laundry,* she thought.

With great effort, she lifted her phone from the nightstand and pulled it close to her face. It was half past ten. If she had woken up this late on a normal day, she would have flung herself out of bed and rushed to get ready as fast as she possibly could. But today, she sat on the edge of her bed, slipped her robe over her pajamas, and slid her feet into slippers. Ignoring the time, she began tidying her room—throwing away all small pieces of trash, picking up various items on the floor, and gathering her laundry so she could toss in a load. After the washer was running and her room vacuumed, she stood in her doorway admiring her accomplishment.

Unsure if her dad would come back to the house for lunch, she thought it would be best if she wasn't there, just in case. She took a quick shower and pulled her long, wet mop of brown hair into a high bun.

She grabbed her phone from her nightstand and saw a text from Karen.

*So now you and your boyfriend are just skipping school together?*

Jeddie's face burned with irritation. She deleted the text and shoved her phone into her bag. Karen had been accusing Jeddie and Peter of dating the entire term, and Jeddie had decided she wasn't going to fall prey to the drama.

She draped her camera strap over her shoulder, then put her sketchbook into her backpack. In the garage, she slipped her sneakers on before gliding off on her bike. The ride to the next town—Peter's hometown, Mountain View—seemed much quicker this time. She didn't think Peter would react well if he knew she was making a second trip, but she was too curious to see the rest of the house.

She circled neighborhoods a few times before she found the street where Peter's old home was. Not wanting passersby to know someone was at the house, she took her bike around to the side to keep it hidden.

With her camera strapped around her neck, she fiddled with the switches and buttons until she was happy with the settings. There were no cars or pedestrians on the street and she took the opportunity to duck inside the house unnoticed. The front door creaked shut as she pushed it into its frame. Her heart thumped in her chest. It made her nervous to be inside alone. She wasn't sure if it was because she felt like she was invading Peter's life, or because she was breaking into a home she was sure she wasn't allowed to be in. And coming here two days in a row could draw attention from the neighbors.

Not knowing what she was hoping to accomplish, she started to walk around the main floor. From the living room, you could almost see the layout of the entire house. The sheetrock had been burned through, and wall frames were exposed. From where she stood, she could see some of the upper level of the house. The floor had collapsed where she assumed a bedroom once existed. Turning her gaze from the upper level to the level where she stood, she saw what used to be a bed and frame shattered over the kitchen counter.

She began taking pictures of every angle. The shutter of her camera echoed in the abandoned home. Making her way to the kitchen, she tiptoed over wall insulation. The furry pink puffs reminded her of cotton candy. She was paying so much attention to her feet that she nearly hit her head on a pipe that dangled from the ceiling. "Woah," she blurted as she ducked to miss it. Her voice felt loud and made her heart beat faster. She swiveled around, looking in all directions to make sure she was still alone. She had an eerie feeling she was being watched.

She got closer to the bedframe. Stubs of ashy wood protruded out of the frame. Jeddie assumed that the mattress had been completely destroyed, because the only thing left resting on the bed was the metal of the box springs. She turned her head and noticed the house revealed some of the story of the fire. From the living room and kitchen and the entire house to the left of her, the fire damage was extensive. But once she turned to the right, where the dining room and the side of the house where Peter's room was, the house showed minimal damage. From what Jeddie could gather, that part of the house had suffered mostly heat damage.

Jeddie focused her camera on the contrast. She backed to the far end of the kitchen where she could see both the kitchen and the dining room. The burned, black wallpaper from the kitchen bled into a faded green floral design that covered the dining room. Light from the upper floor shone down onto the bed that now rested in the workspace of the kitchen. Only spots of linoleum flooring could be seen where she stood, then, on the other side of the archway leading to the dining room, ragged edges of the flooring began again. A rainbow spew of melted-then-hardened crayons covered part of the dining room table.

The floorboard creaked under her foot as she made her way to the bubble of crayon. Her fingers glided around the edges, revealing rich colors of wax underneath particles of dust. Peter's childhood now lingering in ashes made her feel sick, the effect it must have had on Peter starting to sink in. Standing in his old home, taking in all the damage, she realized that the perfect memories Peter had of this place were taken away the instant they had pulled up on their bikes the day before.

A feeling of guilt for being in the house sat heavy in the pit of her stomach. She turned to leave out of the doorway on the other side of the dining room, which opened into the back of the hallway that led to Peter's room and the front door. She was enticed to look in Peter's room once more. Her abrupt exit the day before hadn't allowed her to see his room in detail, but now, standing in it, she noticed a few of the figurines had since been placed atop the melted walls. The afternoon sun shone directly onto the Lego castle and Jeddie couldn't help but snap a few photos.

A broken picture frame lay on the floor by the dresser. Shattered pieces of glass fell to the floor as she picked it up. Running her fingers over the cardboard square that was used to hold the photo in place, she tried to imagine what picture had been in the frame. As she flipped it over, the backside revealed a note that simply said,

*Love,*
*Mom*

SHE HURRIED and set the frame on the floor with the words face-up. Her camera snapped as she caught the handwriting of Peter's mom. After capturing the final shots of Peter's room, she put the lens cover on her camera. She smiled to herself as she fastened the strap around her shoulder again and headed out of the room, more careful this time as she crouched underneath the banister and tiptoed around the chandelier. With one last glance down the hallway, she ducked out the front door, somewhat grateful to get rid of the eerie feeling she'd had in the house.

Before she could turn to get her bike from the side of the house, she stopped dead in her tracks on the porch looking out to the street. An unexpected visitor was watching her as she came out of the house.

"Hello, Jeddie," the woman said in a drawn-out voice. "I'm Elaine. I think we should chat."

## 9

J eddie hesitated on the porch while Elaine stared at her. She was leaning backward on an angle against her truck. Her arms were folded, but she didn't seem mad. Jeddie wasn't sure if the "chat" Elaine wanted to have was a good thing or a bad thing.

"Come, on." Elaine motioned Jeddie to get in the truck. "Grab your bike."

Jeddie looked to the side of the house in surprise. She had assumed her bike was well hidden, but apparently not to the observant. With shame, she wheeled the orange bike to the back of truck and lifted it into the bed with Elaine's help.

Each of them pulled themselves up by the truck's ceiling handle and into their seats. They simultaneously pulled their doors shut.

Jeddie asked the question she had been wondering from the moment she saw Elaine outside the house. "How did you know where the house was?"

"Peter told me the general area. After I dropped him off late at school, I decided to come check it out myself." She chuckled to herself before adding, "To be honest, I drove around the neighborhoods for about an hour before I found it. I walked around the yard when I first got here, and that's when I saw what I knew must be your bike. I figured it would be best to wait outside for you, instead of frightening you by barging into the house."

Jeddie didn't say anything, just stared out the passenger window, looking at the garage where the roof had collapsed.

"It took him a while to open up, but Peter told me about yesterday," Elaine continued.

Jeddie's head dropped, a mixture of shame and guilt.

"He feels awful that he yelled at you." Elaine paused, as if waiting for Jeddie to say something, but Jeddie stayed silent. After a moment, Elaine said, "You have to understand that this whole thing really shocked Peter."

Jeddie nodded. "I know."

"He really idealized this home. I think there was this huge part of him that always hoped he and his mom would leave Lakewood one day and come back here, start where they'd left off and continue a normal life."

Elaine shifted in her seat so she was angled toward Jeddie. "I don't think it is easy for any of us to quite understand what Peter has gone through. We might be able to sympathize with him on a few things, but the overall picture of his life is so unique that our sympathy will never equate to empathy."

Jeddie hadn't turned to look at Elaine. She was getting sick to her stomach and fought back tears.

"Jeddie, I want you to know that I think you are the best thing that has happened to Peter in a long time. He has really needed a friend. And though it was tough for him to come here yesterday, I think it will give him the push he needs to finally move on from this idealized life he has made up in his head."

Jeddie finally turned and met Elaine's eyes. She had a gentle, encouraging smile. Jeddie was surprised that she wasn't upset with her. "I just hope he'll still want to be friends. You know, he has been really important to me too. I don't think I realized that until yesterday."

"Then it's a good thing that you both want to be friends still."

"I'm not so sure Peter wants that. He was so mad."

"I'm sure," Elaine said as she put her hand on Jeddie's shoulder and looked her straight in the eye. "Because he told me."

Jeddie felt her tough outer appearance collapse. "I'm really glad." She slid to the middle of the front seat to give Elaine a hug. "Thank you."

Elaine wrapped her arms around her. "I will say, Jeddie, you are a strong young woman. I know you haven't had the easiest childhood either. I think that is what makes you and Peter the perfect friends. You can certainly lean on each other."

Elaine held onto her for a long time before appearing to notice the camera strapped around Jeddie's neck. "Do you mind if I take a look?" she asked, pointing at the camera.

"Of course not."

They both stared at the digital screen of the camera as Elaine clicked through the photos. Each one seemed to surprise Elaine more than the previous. Every time she came to a new photo, she let out a gasp, "Oh my...That's just awful..." When she came across the picture of the Lego house, she paused. "Did Peter build this?"

"Yeah. It's pretty amazing, isn't it?"

"Yeah, it is." She zoomed in, taking a closer look at the detail. "He's a pretty amazing kid."

"Elaine?" Jeddie sat up straight in her seat, an idea suddenly taking shape in her mind.

"Yeah?"

"Do you think you could help me with something?"

"What's that?"

"Well, a couple of weeks ago, Peter had dinner at my house and he couldn't stop mentioning how much he loved the landscaping. He said it reminded him of the Lakewood grounds, which were pretty much the only thing he liked about that place."

Elaine seemed to catch on to what Jeddie was hinting at. "I don't know if that's a good idea, Jeddie."

"You haven't let me finish."

Elaine gave her a look of defeat. "Okay, go on."

"Every year, my dad likes to find a landscaping charity project, a project that we do for free for someone. Would you be okay if I ran it by him to see if we can make your yard this year's project? I think that would mean a lot to Peter."

Elaine twisted her lips, looking unsure. "You and Peter seem to have the same idea. But it's just not that easy for me. I am so embarrassed about my backyard."

"Please?" Jeddie continued.

"Okay, you can ask, but if I'm going to let you do this, it has to be on my terms. I want it to be a surprise to Peter, so he can't know anything about this. Got it?"

"Absolutely." Jeddie grinned, and Elaine quickly returned it.

~

ELAINE PULLED up to the front of the nursery. Jeddie looked at her, begging with her eyes to drive to the back and drop her off at home.

"You need to tell your dad where you've been today."

"But, why? Nothing happened."

"Jeddie, you skipped school. Your dad will find out eventually and it will be better if you come clean now."

"It was a one-time thing. I won't do it again."

"That sounds like a good thing to convince your dad of."

Jeddie let out a grunt.

"Go on," Elaine nudged.

"Okay, fine."

She grabbed her belongings and jumped out of the truck. Elaine waited while she lifted her bike onto the asphalt of the parking lot. Jeddie rested her arm on the open passenger side window.

"Thanks for the ride."

"You bet, kiddo."

"And the talk," Jeddie added.

Elaine gave her a smile and a wave as she pulled out of the parking lot. Jeddie wheeled her bike to the door of her dad's office.

Kent's office was quiet when Jeddie walked in. She assumed Kent must be out helping customers and used the extra time to gather her thoughts on how she was going to explain the fact that she had skipped school.

She plopped down onto the couch and took the strap of her camera off her neck. For the second time that day, she scrolled through the pictures she had taken at Peter's home until she came to the last picture of his mom's signature. She stared at the picture, mesmerized, until Kent came in.

"Sweetheart," he said, surprised. "How was your day?"

She looked at him, trying to understand if it was just his normal asking, or if he was digging for answers.

"It was good."

"You learn anything interesting today?"

*He's digging for information.* "Elaine told you?"

"She wanted to make sure you came clean, but then gave me a lecture on giving you the benefit of the doubt."

"I'm sorry, Dad. I woke up late."

"I know." He rolled his chair over to the couch. "But that's no excuse for cutting school."

Jeddie gave him small nods. "I don't know why I did it. But when I woke up, I just didn't think I could fake my way through school today with a happy face."

"You can't skip out on life when things are hard or awkward. Trust me. I've done that, and it doesn't always work out." He bent his head down until they were making eye contact. "I expect more from you. And I hope you expect more from yourself."

"I do."

"All right then. Go put your work clothes on. You're with me the rest of the day."

"Dad, I have to go get caught up from all the work I missed today."

"Well, you should have thought about that before skipping school. Looks like you'll have extra work this weekend."

Jeddie went to protest, but Kent interrupted. "Come on. Get going." Kent pointed to the door. "Be back in ten minutes."

She continued her act of annoyance out the door, but deep down, time with her dad was exactly what she needed.

After a quick change of clothes, she made it back to her dad's office. She let out a small laugh of disbelief when he led her around the front of the nursery. A delivery truck was pulling up, and he was making it her job to help unload.

After emptying the truck of soil bags, pots, boxes of garden chemicals, and other miscellaneous items, she found her way to a bench down the pebble pathway and sat down, tired and sweaty. Kent walked over and nudged her foot. He waved his hand, gesturing for her to scoot over and make room.

They sat in silence and watched customers look at plant tags, careful to pick the right one for their yard.

Jeddie broke the silence when she remembered her conversation with Elaine. "Hey, Dad?"

"Yeah?"

"You know how we do a charity project every year, designing and landscaping someone's yard for free?"

"Yes," he answered.

"I was talking to Elaine about Peter, and something he keeps mentioning is how impressed he was with our backyard."

"Okay..."

"Well from what Peter has told me, Elaine's backyard could really use some help. I was thinking that maybe her yard could be our charity project this year. What do you think?"

Kent thought for a minute before answering. "Yeah, I think we could do that."

"For real?" Jeddie asked excitedly.

"You bet." Kent turned on the bench to face her. "Maybe we could even incorporate it into your school project. Would you like that?"

"That would be awesome."

"Great. I'll see if there's a time Elaine will let us come

take measurements of the yard, and then we can start sketching the design next week."

"That's so cool. Thanks, Dad."

"You're welcome. Now come on," he said, standing up. "We've got more work to do."

## 10

After school ended the next day, Jeddie met the rest of the track and field team outside. Karen was with a group of girls stretching near the bleachers, getting ready to take off on their long-distance run. Jeddie used to be good friends with the girls, but when she and Karen had their falling out, all of them had taken Karen's side.

"Look everyone, Peter's girlfriend decided to show up," Karen sneered.

Jeddie walked passed her, ignoring her comment.

"Now you're too good for us?" Karen continued.

"No," Jeddie answered, annoyed.

"Well, I have to say, I just don't see it. You and Peter, I mean. I wouldn't have ever pinned *you* as his type," Karen demeaned.

"It's a good thing we're not a couple then." Jeddie finished her stretches then took off on her run.

"Hey, you're supposed to wait for us," Karen yelled after her, but Jeddie kept going.

She sprinted to the street, her feet thumping against the

concrete with each stride. She replayed Karen's words in her mind. Today's comments, built on an entire year of other catty comments, made Jeddie's adrenaline kick in. She ran harder than she usually did, her mind filled with things she wished she could say to Karen. Comebacks that would defend Peter. But she knew if she told Karen anything, she would betray Peter's trust.

Sweat dripped off her forehead as she stopped at the corner of a busy intersection. Bending over, she rested her hands on her knees to catch her breath. It wasn't until she stood back up that she realized she had no idea where she was. Her eyes jutted back and forth in all directions as she turned in circles, feeling completely lost. None of the nearby buildings or landmarks looked familiar to her. Looking down at her watch, she realized she had been running for over an hour, and hadn't paid any attention to where she was going; now she had no idea where she was. She sat on top of a green electrical box and closed her eyes. The thud of tires running over bumps in the road filled her ears as cars sped past her.

She tried to remember all the turns she had made to end up where she was, but her mind had been too preoccupied thinking about Karen. With determination, she got up again and kept running, too upset to worry about being lost. Using the surrounding mountains as her guide, she turned and headed north, figuring as long as she knew where the mountains were, she would eventually make it home.

With each stride, the street became calmer, less crowded. Her mind started to slow, and she paced herself to a jog. As she passed another corner, the street name— Lassiter Avenue—caught her attention and made her stop. It took her a minute, but her eyes widened with excitement when she remembered how she knew that street name. All of her research she had been doing for their term project always came back to one place. She broke into a sprint, passing a few more streets until she found the street name she was looking for: Lakewood Drive.

She panted as she looked upward. The incline of the street was steep, and she braced herself for the climb. She had been so curious about Lakewood and couldn't believe she was finally going to see it. Her excitement grew with each step as she made her way around the bend at the top of the hill and everything came into view. When she caught her breath, she realized she was resting her hand on a concrete sign that read "Lakewood Residence Center."

WHILE THE KIDS were at school, Kent had snuck to Elaine's house to measure her backyard. Jeddie had warned him about the condition of Elaine's yard, so he would be prepared when he saw it. But when Elaine let him through the back gate, his jaw dropped in disbelief.

"I know, it's terrible," she said, sounding ashamed.

Kent looked around in awe. He hadn't realized how big of an undertaking he'd agreed to until he saw how overgrown and out-of-sorts the backyard was. Overwhelmed, he trudged his way through vines and weeds. When he'd made his way to the middle of the yard, waist deep in weeds, he turned back to look at Elaine, the woman who inspired him to become a landscape architect. She was sitting on her patio bench, slouched over, her head resting in her hands.

Kent dug his way back and sat down next to her. "Hey, we're going to figure this out. Everything will be okay."

"I know. I'm just so embarrassed to show you my yard. My star student, nonetheless."

Kent, not wanting her to feel worse than he could tell she already did, thought carefully how to word his thoughts. "Can I ask how your yard got this way?"

She shrugged her shoulders. "Neglect."

"But you...you, of all people, taught me how important it is to keep up on yard work. What happened?"

"It became something at the bottom of my priorities." Tears started to form in her eyes. "My husband, Larry, became extremely ill, and all of my energy was reserved for taking care of him."

"But the front yard..."

"I wanted people to believe that I was doing all right. And for the most part, it's worked."

"Elaine, I'm so sorry."

"Me too. Watching my husband die is the hardest thing I have ever gone through."

Kent took her hand in both of his. Out of all of his college professors, Elaine had made the biggest impact on him. Her love for all things plants and landscaping piqued his interest. It crushed him, knowing that she had become sad enough to let her passion fade.

"I think it's time we ignite your love for this yard again," he suggested. "What do you say?"

"You're probably right."

"Then let's get measuring!" He stood up and held out a hand to help her up off the bench.

Although he was certain the gutting of the yard could be done in a day, the task of installing the yard that same day was daunting. But in order to ensure that it would remain a surprise for Peter, it would need to be done.

With Elaine's help, he got the measurements he needed and made a rough sketch of the shape of the yard.

"If you think of any special requests for the yard, just

give me a call," Kent assured. He pulled Elaine in and gave her a hug. "Thank you for letting me be a part of this."

"Thank you for not judging me."

"Oh, I'm judging, just on the inside." He let out a chuckle and winked at her.

BACK AT THE NURSERY, Kent and Jeddie each sat at their sketch tables. Jeddie always wanted to help with the design of their yearly charity project. Kent gave her the measurements and they each made a rough sketch with their ideas.

It took a week of sketching and coordinating with Kent's team before the final plan came together. They concluded that, in order to get the entire yard gutted, leveled, brick paths laid, and landscaped, they would need to start around four in the morning.

The night before their project took place, Kent, Jeddie, and the crew crowded in Kent's office to coordinate all of the work to be done. Since this project had been Jeddie's idea, Kent had let her lead on almost everything. Seeing her in front, leading the crew, made him proud.

IN THE MORNING, Elaine crept into Peter's room.

"Peter," she said, gently shaking his shoulder.

It only took the one shake for Peter to jolt awake. He shot up to sitting when he saw Elaine.

"Sorry, I didn't mean to scare you," she said.

"What's going on?" he asked through a yawn.

"I've planned a whole day for us. Come on. Get dressed."

"What time is it?"

"Pretty early...Hurry up, I'll be waiting in the kitchen."

Soon after, Peter stumbled down the stairs, and Elaine guided him to her car. Right before she pulled out of the driveway, she sent a text to Jeddie, letting her know the coast would be clear in two minutes.

HIDDEN in the dark of the early morning, the crew was on stand-by, waiting in their vehicles a block away, when the text came in from Elaine. The crew drove up to the house and began to unload their equipment.

Flood lights lit the yard while the crew started their work. Backhoes and heavy machinery were brought in to help gut the yard. Jeddie watched excitedly as section after section of weeds were pulled and hauled off. Two hours into their time, the yard had been completely gutted, and the sun started to rise.

"Well, how about that?" Kent said to Jeddie.

She gave him a smile and side hug. "Pretty amazing."

ELAINE TOOK Peter to an all-hours pancake shop. With a groggy voice, he barely made it through ordering his breakfast. Because she was trying to take up time, Elaine convinced him to order the all-you-can-eat pancake breakfast.

"You'd better wake up, kiddo. We got a long day ahead of us."

"We do?" he asked, yawning again.

"Yep."

Though they were the only customers in the restaurant,

Elaine somehow managed to drag breakfast on for an hour and a half. When Peter finished his second plate, Elaine asked the waitress for another round.

"Really, Elaine, I'm stuffed. Please don't make me eat any more."

She wasn't paying attention to what Peter said. She was looking down at her watch and shaking her head. She had been having so much fun dragging breakfast out that she overdid it. "Oh no, we're going to be late. We'd better get going."

Elaine stood up and pulled her wallet out to pay.

"But you just ordered another plate of pancakes," Peter said groggily.

Standing at the front register, she waved Peter over. "Come on, we're going to miss it if we don't hurry."

"Miss what?"

She didn't answer, instead just headed out the door and beckoned him to follow. They got into the car and Elaine started the engine, pulling out of the lot the second Peter buckled his seatbelt.

She drove along the edge of town, opposite her home, and up the mountainside before coming to a parking lot that looked out over the city. She backed into one of the spaces so the bed of the truck faced the view. She got out and lowered the door of the truck bed, lifting herself up and motioning for Peter to join her.

Building lights faded as the morning sun started to rise. Beams of white sunlight peaked through mountain ranges. It was quiet, but not an uncomfortable or lonely quiet. This quiet was peaceful; Elaine felt renewed, and hoped that Peter did too.

"I used to come up here with Larry," Elaine said, breaking the silence. "When he was diagnosed, sometimes it was good to take him away from it all—the doctors, treat-ments, being inside. I felt like it was a good escape for both of us." She could feel Peter watching her intently; she didn't open up about Larry often. "Sometimes, when I am really missing him, I find myself sitting here either watching the sun rise or set, and I always leave feeling a little better."

They sat in silence for a long time, feeling the warm sun on their cheeks and closing their eyes while it continued to rise higher in the sky.

"If you ever feel like you need a minute to get away from all the things you are going through, this is a good place," Elaine said.

"Thank you for bringing me here," Peter replied. He gave her a smile and she patted him on the shoulder.

After another thirty minutes, Elaine was onto the next adventure of the day. She and Peter got back in the truck and were on their way again.

"It's been almost an hour, Elaine. Where in the world are we going?" Peter asked.

Elaine laughed, not willing to let him in on the secret. "You'll see soon enough."

AFTER A SHORT BREAK, the team assembled to look at the design one last time before they went to work. Kent had loads of new soil brought in; fresh soil was needed to give every plant the best chance of survival.

When the yard was leveled out, the team assembled landscaping bricks around the flowerbeds and hand laid stone pathways. Jeddie couldn't help but smile when the pathways were laid. Those alone made the yard look beautiful.

She helped bring around the sod and rolled it out. When the grass was installed, she and Kent stepped onto the patio together to take a look at their progress.

"I can't believe this is actually coming together," Jeddie said.

"To be honest, I'm surprised too. I definitely had my doubts."

"Peter is going to love this."

"Yeah. But you know who will love this more? Elaine." He looked at her with a big grin.

ELAINE PULLED into the parking lot of their destination, and Peter looked at her, surprised.

"The zoo?" Peter asked.

"Shall we?" she said, seemingly unfazed by his question.

After buying their tickets, they stood inside the entrance.

"I haven't been to the zoo in forever," Peter said when they started walking.

"Do you remember the last time?"

"Yeah. Actually, I found a picture of that day in my old house."

"Really?"

"Yeah. It was part of my birthday present that year."

Elaine looked relieved that Peter's last memory of the zoo was a happy one. She must have seen him stewing over his map and asked, "You know where you want to go first?"

"I don't know, it all looks good. Let's go to the right and make the circle around the park."

They were lucky to have arrived close to opening time. It seemed as if they had the place to themselves. Each exhibit was wide open and they had time to watch the animals uninterrupted by others blocking their view.

Peter loved watching the seals and penguins swim and do tricks. At first, he thought he could stay and watch all the animals for hours, but after each exhibit, an uneasy feeling kept growing in him. It wasn't until later in the afternoon that he realized where the uneasy feeling was coming from.

The afternoon rush of people had started to gather and they fought their way through the crowds. The exhibit of the orangutans was grassy with several wooden climbing structures. Everyone was gathered around the fence, watching.

"Wow. Look at that one," a boy from the crowd said.

Peter's gaze turned in the direction of where the boy had pointed. A large orangutan sat on the base of one of the wooden structures, turning a ball over and over in his hand.

Watching the ball being turned over and over flashed Peter back to the Lakewood. He pictured himself turning his baseball in his hand, sitting on the edge of his bed, just wishing he could go outside. Waiting for someone to allow him out of his room. Now, on the outside watching the orangutan in the cage, he felt like a hypocrite.

He turned around and made his way to a bench across the walkway. Elaine, still watching, hadn't noticed he had walked away until minutes later.

"Hey, you. What are you doing over here?" She sat next to him.

"Can we go?"

"Go? There's still so much to see."

"I want to go home."

"What happened? You were fine just a little bit ago."

"Nothing, I just want to go home."

"Peter," she said simply. The look she gave him let him know she wasn't buying his lie.

"That monkey with the ball just reminded me of being at Lakewood. I used to sit on my bed with a baseball all the time, counting the seconds until someone finally came and got me. And it feels a little hypocritical now, standing on the outside of the cage looking in."

Elaine gave him a sympathetic look. "Peter, you being here at the zoo is nothing compared to your mom locking you up in that hospital."

"It feels exactly like that."

"Honey, I know it must be weird for you to suddenly be immersed back into the functional world outside of the hospital, but if I could wish anything upon you, it would be that you wouldn't feel guilty for the normal experiences you get to have now."

Peter didn't respond, so Elaine continued.

"If you always dwell on the past, it will be impossible to live a full life in the future." She stood from the bench. "Now, I brought you here, and we are not leaving until we see that butterfly exhibit."

That got a smile out of him. He hopped up from the bench and followed her. He couldn't help but think that Elaine always knew how to make him feel better.

JEDDIE RECEIVED A TEXT FROM ELAINE, warning her and the crew that they were leaving the zoo and would be back to the house in a little over an hour. The crew had been working hard to ensure they could be finished and cleaned up before Elaine and Peter came home.

Jeddie looked around the yard and couldn't believe the

progress they had made in one day. Though they were unable to build the overhang for the patio, or install the fire pit, the rest of the yard was completely finished. She couldn't wait to see Peter's reaction.

The crew hauled all their tools to their trucks, then moved their vehicles a block away so Peter would be completely surprised.

ELAINE'S TRUCK puttered in the driveway until she turned the key. Peter, exhausted from being woken up so early that morning, had fallen asleep on the way home. When Elaine shut off the car, the abrupt stop of the rattling engine woke Peter up.

"Sorry, I didn't mean to fall asleep," he said.

"That's quite all right."

"Thanks for everything today."

"You bet, kiddo," Elaine said, peering around the side of the house at something Peter couldn't see. "But there is one more surprise in store."

Peter looked at her, puzzled.

"Come on." She jumped out of the car and went inside the house, Peter following close behind.

Leading him through the kitchen, Elaine stopped where the sliding glass door overlooked the yard. Without saying anything, she nodded her head toward the door and motioned him to look out back.

He walked over and together they took in the new yard. Peter's jaw dropped as he tried to process the total transformation.

"For real? How did this happen?" he asked.

"Why don't you go see?" Elaine replied, and pulled the door open so they could both walk onto the deck.

Jeddie, Kent, and the crew were waiting for them.

The whole crew yelled "surprise!" in unison.

"This was all her idea," Elaine said, pointing at Jeddie.

They joined the crew down on the lawn. Each crewmember wanted to show them the details they had been working on. They pointed to different trees and shrubs, and were most excited about the seating on the new stone patio where Peter and Elaine could enjoy the coming summer nights.

Finally, Peter approached Jeddie and Kent. "I can't believe you guys. This is incredible."

"It was all Jeddie's idea," Kent said.

"Well, I couldn't have done it without him." Jeddie gave Kent a side hug.

Peter and Jeddie sat on the patio bench, enjoying the hard work that was put in. "This really is amazing, Jeddie."

"I'm glad you like it."

EVENTUALLY THE CREW DISPERSED, leaving the four of them. Kent walked over to Elaine in the corner of the yard. She was looking at a red-leafed Japanese Maple tree.

"What do you think, Professor?"

She turned to him, tears in her eyes. "I don't know what to say. This is amazing, Kent, really."

"I learned everything I know from you."

"I'm so grateful for everything you have done for Peter. And now this," she said, looking around the yard. "Thank you."

"You're welcome," he said and gave her a hug.

"How can I repay you?"

"You don't have to do anything."

"The least I can do is feed you," Elaine insisted.

She was halfway up the deck stairs when she beckoned them inside.

"Come on, you two," Kent said to Jeddie and Peter. "Elaine insists on feeding us."

Kent and Jeddie both took off their work boots and carried them to the front porch.

"Make yourselves at home," Elaine said. "I'm just going to put together some sandwiches. You guys must be starving after the day you've had."

Kent tried to lend a hand, but Elaine shooed him out of the kitchen and told him to relax in the living room.

The kids followed him in where Peter plopped on the couch. Jeddie and Kent started looking at pictures on the wall.

"Are these all your grandkids, Elaine?" Jeddie asked.

"Most of them. The older pictures are of me and my siblings growing up."

She took a closer look, probably noticing the funny haircuts.

Kent had taken the opposite loop and was looking at pictures above and on the piano. He noticed a man in uniform and figured it must have been Elaine's husband. When he came to a picture on the end of the piano, he picked it up to take a closer look.

His eyes widened. "Who is the little boy in this picture?" He held it up to show Elaine.

"That's Peter." She pointed her mayonnaise-glazed knife at the boy in question.

Kent whipped around. "Peter, how do you know the woman in this picture?"

"That's my mom."

"Your mom?"

Peter nodded.

Kent reached up and ran a hand down his face. Shakily, he put the frame back on the piano. "I don't believe I ever asked you your last name. What is it?"

"Doyle."

He felt his face drain.

"You okay, Dad?" he distantly heard Jeddie ask.

"Um, yeah."

Elaine looked concerned. "Is everything okay?"

"Yeah, I'm just...I'm not feeling well all of a sudden."

Without another word, he walked out the front door and shut it behind him. He didn't turn back to glance at the window where he was sure Jeddie was watching. Kent got into his truck and slammed the door. He started the engine, and clenched the steering wheel tightly with both hands, shaking his head. Needing time to think and knowing Jeddie was in good hands with Elaine, he shifted into gear and drove off.

## 11

"So what game did you end up playing today, Peter?" Margie asked as Peter came to the reception desk. Occasionally, Lisa would allow Peter to play games with the patients. On days when Lisa was busy, he would sneak over to talk with Margie.

"Checkers."

Peter was twelve; he and Lisa had been living at Lakewood for four years.

"The whole time? That's a long game of checkers."

"Better than being in my room."

Margie frowned. "You want to go to the cafeteria and get some ice cream?"

Peter nodded.

Before they left the reception desk, they heard Lisa talking around the corner. "Okay, I will do that and be right back." Her footsteps drew closer.

Peter hurried and ducked underneath the desk, barely making it before Lisa rounded the corner.

"Margie, have you seen Peter?"

"I thought he was playing games with the patients," Margie replied calmly.

"He's not there. He must be back in his room. I haven't been able to walk back there and check."

Peter crunched his knees closer to his chest. *Please don't tell her,* he thought.

Lisa's phone chimed and she looked at it, frustrated. "Ugh."

"Is everything all right?"

"Uh, yep. I just need to go get something from my car."

Margie didn't acknowledge him until Lisa's footsteps had fully faded away. She pushed her chair away from her desk until it wheeled far enough for her to see Peter's face.

"You'd better skedaddle before she gets back," she said.

Peter hurried down the hall to his room. Frustrated, he threw himself onto his bed. He hated being locked up. *I hate this place*, he thought as he laid there.

His head shot up when he heard muffled voices outside his window and got up to see who it was. When he saw that it was his mom, he instinctively backed away from the window, far enough that if his mom were to look up, she wouldn't see him standing there. He inched over to the wall adjacent to the window and peeked his head over.

Lisa was talking to a man Peter had never seen before. They were arguing. He wished he was able to crack his window open to hear what they were saying, but for safety precautions, the windows were sealed.

The man looked like he was pleading with Lisa. There was something in his hand, and to Peter's best guess, it was a picture. The man kept holding it in front of Lisa, and finally, seeming fed up, she shoved his hand away.

The man slouched his shoulders and dropped his head before turning his back and getting into his car. Lisa stood still as he pulled out of the parking lot. When he was out of sight, she turned on her heel and marched inside.

Peter pulled away from the window and grabbed a book off the shelf. He barely made it to his desk with the book opened before Lisa threw open the door.

Peter tried to act casual, not wanting Lisa to know he had seen her arguing with the man outside.

"Hey, kid. You ready for some lunch?"

He looked up from his book to see a big smile on Lisa's face. It was unusual. In fact, Peter couldn't remember the last time he saw her smile, and it was unsettling.

He played along. "Yeah, I'm starving."

"I thought we would head to the cafeteria together. We could get some sheet cake for dessert. How does that sound?"

Peter didn't know whether or not to be relieved that she was putting on a good act. But if she was going to put on an act, he decided it would be best if he did too.

His mom put her arm around him as they walked, almost skipped, down the hallway. She hugged him tightly when they entered the cafeteria door and told him to fill his plate with anything he wanted today.

When he stayed put, she gave him a reassuring nudge. He stood there, watching her, before filling his plate. For that small moment, it felt as if it was just the two of them back in their house. She used to be so gentle and loving. It was a feeling he hadn't felt in a long time.

KENT'S SPEEDOMETER was creeping up toward fifty miles per hour on a back residential road. He was laser focused on getting back to his office and somehow made it to the nursery without getting pulled over. He knew Jeddie would be upset that he left her at Elaine's, but he needed time to process. His face started to get hot, his jaw tight.

Getting out of his truck, he stomped to his office door, shutting and locking it behind him. He threw his keys on his desk and yanked open the bottom drawer of his filing cabinet in the corner of the room. He frantically flipped through files until he came to a blank, unlabeled manila folder.

Shaking, he wheeled to his desk and placed the open folder in front of him.

"Please tell me I'm wrong," he said out loud.

Only one thing was in the folder: a newspaper article. He picked it up and looked it over and over. It depicted a house fire.

"No. It can't be." He stood and began pacing the room. "There's no way she would do this." He rubbed his hand over his mouth as he processed his thoughts.

He pulled his phone out of his pocket and dialed a number that he hadn't for over three years.

His heart beat faster with each ring. Voicemail. *"You have reached Lisa Doyle. Please leave a message at the tone."*

Immediately, he dialed again.

"Come on...Pick up, pick up..."

*"You have reached Lisa Doyle. Please leave a mess—"* He hung up.

He flung the phone onto the desk and continued to pace the floor. He could feel his heart beating in his chest, and he stumbled to his chair to gather himself. His hand shook as he lifted it up to his mouth and wiped away the cold sweat dripping down his face, a nauseated feeling coming over him. Just in case, he grabbed his trash can and hunched over it. Taking deep breaths in and out, only one thought entered his mind. *There's no way she would do this, right?*

KENT SAT with his head in the palms of his hands until the nausea subsided. Then, to clear his mind, he walked to the washroom that had a deep plastic utility sink and put his head under the faucet. The cold water felt refreshing on his face and neck as he let it run over him for several minutes. With his head still under the faucet, he reached for the handle to turn the sink off.

He let the cool water drip into the sink and then ran his fingers through his hair to shake off the excess. He grabbed a clean work towel off the stack he kept on the counter to wipe his face and ears, then pressed both palms into the counter, leaning on it and adjusting his weight to one leg.

Still not wanting to give in to what he was thinking, he cocked his head to the side as another thought entered his mind. With small beads of water still running down his neck, he hurried back to his desk and pulled the newspaper article out again. He scribbled a few notes on a pad of paper, then carefully slid the article back into the folder and into the filing cabinet.

AFTER KENT HAD DRIVEN OFF, Jeddie, Elaine, and Peter had looked at one another, baffled. Kent's leaving was so abrupt that they really hadn't processed what it was that had made him leave. The three of them sat at the kitchen table eating the sandwiches Elaine had made. There was no reason to let them go to waste just because Kent had left. Jeddie sat facing the living room and couldn't help but stare at the photo of Peter and his mom. Peter kept looking at Elaine, as if in hopes she would tell him what they should do.

Jeddie took huge bites, barely chewing before gulping them down. Then she politely excused herself from the table.

She walked over to the piano to get a closer look at the photo. Jeddie guessed that Peter was about eight or nine when the picture was taken. She stared at his mom, leaning in to get a closer look at her face. She wanted to see if she recognized her. In the picture, her blonde hair barely grazed her shoulders. Her genuine smile brought wrinkles around her eyes. Her arm rested on Peter's shoulder, as they had both leaned in, giving each other a side hug. Looking one last time into her eyes, it dawned on Jeddie that she had seen this woman before. She had seen her recently.

Her eyes widened as she took the frame in her hands.

"What is it, Jeddie?" Peter asked, still sitting at the kitchen table.

She looked up from the picture. "What?" she asked, trying to act coy.

"You okay?"

"Mmhmm," she said, nodding her head. "Elaine, would you be able to give me a ride home?"

Despite Jeddie's act, Elaine must have suspected something was bothering her. "You sure you're all right?" she asked.

"Yeah, I'm sure."

Before Elaine had dropped Jeddie off at home, they'd driven by the nursery. Jeddie, though still confused about her dad's sudden, unexplained departure, was at least relieved that he was safe. Jeddie sat at her kitchen counter, working on a math problem waiting for Kent to come home.

It had been such a long day that she was having trouble staying awake. By the time 9:00 p.m. rolled around, she was ready to give up on waiting. When she finally stood up from the stool and packed up her books, Kent walked through the garage door.

"Where have you been?" Jeddie demanded.

"The nursery."

Jeddie looked at him, unimpressed.

"What? That's where I was," he said defensively.

"Did you even realize that you left me at Elaine's?"

Kent felt terrible. "I'm so sorry, sweetie."

"What happened? You seemed totally fine, and then you just left."

"I wasn't feeling well."

"Don't lie to me."

"Okay, look...There was something that was just a little bit of a blast from the past that upset me today."

"What was it?" Jeddie wasn't going to let him off the hook.

"I can't tell you that. I need some more time to work through it. And for all I know, I could be blowing things out of proportion. I really need to verify a few things before I bring you into it. Okay?"

"I guess."

Kent pulled her in for a hug, squeezing so hard she could barely breath. "Everything is going to be okay."

Jeddie wanted more than anything to tell Kent that she'd recognized the woman in the photo with Peter. But if she admitted that, then she would have to explain why she recognized her. She thought back to her run a few days earlier, when, at the top of the hill, Jeddie had stood by the concrete sign of Lakewood Residence Center...

IN AWE, Jeddie walked through the parking lot and onto the front lawn. From what she could see, Lakewood was the only building on top of the hill. Each of the windows had two sets of bars on the outside—one set running vertically and the other horizontally. She walked to the side of the building where a chain-link fence blocked off the back grounds of the facility. She let out a gasp of amazement. Peter had talked about how beautiful the grounds were, and he was right; they were breathtaking. Ducks glided across the lake, which sat at the bottom of a massive granite mountain. An oak tree that looked at least one hundred years old sheltered the grounds with shade. Benches had been built along the walkway so people could sit and enjoy the scenery. Jeddie wanted to take a picture and reached into her pocket, forgetting that her phone was back in the locker room at school.

She jumped behind a tree when she heard a voice coming from the front of the building.

"I understand that, but isn't there something you can do?" the woman said into her phone. "It's been three months—don't you think I deserve to see my son?" She slid her sunglasses through the front of her short, blonde hair and onto her ears. "Well that just doesn't seem right. Isn't there something you can do? They can't keep him from me forever."

Jeddie peered around the tree to see the woman. By the sound of the phone conversation, she assumed it was Peter's mom and wanted to get a good look at her. She approached her car in its reserved spot, which turned out to be right in front of where Jeddie was. Before she could duck back behind the tree again, Jeddie and Peter's mom locked eyes.

"I, uh...I'm going to have to call you back," she said to the person on the phone. She hung up and continued to stare at Jeddie. "Excuse me..."

"Sorry, I was just leaving. I got lost on my run and saw the mountain..." she lied.

The woman's eyes widened when Jeddie came out from behind the tree. "You're...trespassing."

"I'm so sorry, it won't happen again."

Jeddie speed-walked through the parking lot before she broke into a sprint, trying not to think too hard about how Peter's mom seemed to have recognized her somehow.

A FEW DAYS LATER, Lisa had locked herself in the bathroom at work. She put her hand on her cheek, which was extremely warm. She slid down the wall until she was crouching, and rested her elbows on her knees, holding her phone in both hands. Through blurry vision, she saw the notification that she had missed eight calls from Kent, all from the previous day. She hadn't seen or heard from him since he showed up at Lakewood three years ago. He had shown up at Lakewood and they'd argued in the parking lot.

*Something's not right.* Dread of her worst nightmare coming true overcame her.

A prompt popped up on her screen to call him back and she quickly shoved her phone into her scrub pocket.

Two thoughts kept going through her mind: *Either something is wrong with Jeddie, or he knows what I did.*

Her mind stirred. She knew she couldn't ignore Kent forever, but she wasn't ready to find out why he was calling.

A voice on the other side of the bathroom door interrupted her thoughts. "Lisa, is everything okay?"

It was Margie.

"Yes," she said in a raised voice. "Be right out."

She stood at the sink and washed her hands. Her reflection showed black smudges of mascara under her eyes. She rubbed what she could away and decided she couldn't be bothered by the rest.

Before opening the door, she paused, holding the door handle.

*I can do this,* she tried to convince herself. Then, with a confident shove of the door, she walked back to the nurses' station.

Lisa didn't miss Margie eyeing her as she walked over.

"Something going on?" Margie asked.

"Sorry?"

"Everything okay?"

"Oh, yeah." She nodded mechanically. She stood on the patient side of the counter, drumming her fingers. "Hey, will you be all right if I take the rest of the afternoon off? I need to run some errands."

"Yeah, sure." Margie looked at her with suspicion.

Lisa was not accustomed to taking time off. She surprised herself by asking. "Great, you can hold down the fort." She patted the counter twice then, while walking away, said, "I won't be back until tonight."

With keys in hand, and her purse handle falling off her shoulder, she hurried to her car. There was only one place she could think to go, one place she thought Kent would be. As much as she didn't want to see him, she knew that without knowing what he was calling about, her mind would never be at ease.

In the middle of the warm, spring afternoon, traffic was quiet. Lisa made it through town quickly. Her heart started to beat faster and faster as she approached the edge of town and pulled up to Mountain View Cemetery. She let the car glide through the small roads between the graves and slowed to a stop. Just as she had suspected, Kent was there, kneeling down by a grave.

She parked her car and sat there for a minute, watching him. It didn't seem like he had heard her pull up, and she took the time to gather her thoughts. She reasoned that there was a chance she could be overreacting, so it would be best to let him talk first before she let anything slip. Quietly, she got out of her car and walked over to where he was. She stood about ten feet behind him and waited for him to acknowledge her.

"You didn't answer my calls," he said without turning around.

"Sorry, busy at work."

"Don't give me that." He stood and faced her. "We both know you were avoiding my calls. It's been *three years,* Lisa. You know if I'm calling I must have a pretty good reason."

"That's what I'm afraid of."

"You know why I'm here, don't you?"

"I'm hoping not."

He looked at her seriously, fear evident in his eyes. "Please tell me it's not true."

She contemplated what to say. He hadn't confirmed what he was thinking, so she decided to probe. "Tell you what's not true?"

Now he was getting annoyed. "This!" He flung his arm sharply in the direction of the headstone. He knelt by it again, running his fingers over the engraved name.

ANDREW PETER SAMS
IN LOVING MEMORY OF OUR SWEET BOY

"TELL me you wouldn't do this," he said.

"I can't do that." She started to falter. There was no getting around it anymore. Her only option was to try to make him understand. "It was the only way I could make sure he was safe."

"Safe? You've got to be kidding me."

"You caught me off guard. I thought I would never see you again, and then, out of the blue, you call to tell me you're moving back to town. What was I supposed to do?"

"Be a normal person! I wanted to move back so we could try to be a family again."

"A family? Let's not forget who walked out on our family, Kent."

"I just wanted it to stop. You and me. The fighting. We just went around and around in circles. We were both so young and caught up in our own heads. I didn't think it would stop unless we took a break."

"A break? You took off in the middle of the night."

"So...so this was payback?"

"It wasn't that you just left, Kent. You took one kid from me. How was I supposed to guarantee you wouldn't take the other?"

He stood to face her again. "Wow. I knew me leaving had been hard on you, I just didn't think you had gone completely mental."

"I was scared. I did the only thing I could think of to take control of the situation. And if that meant making you think Peter was dead, then so be it."

"You mean Andrew."

"He hasn't gone by Andrew since he was a baby," she

snapped. "I changed his name to Peter Doyle after you left. I didn't want him to go searching for you."

Kent tightened his fists. "So, what, I call you to tell you that Jeddie and I are moving to town so that we can try to be a family again and...and you lose it?"

"Basically." She shrugged her shoulders, tears welling in her eyes.

There was twenty seconds of dead air. Lisa watched Kent processing, his fingers fidgeting at his side.

"Kent, when you left, my whole world shattered. I was a mess." She let out a mirthless laugh. "Even more of a mess than before you left." She took a step toward him. "It took everything in me to build a happy life around Peter and to get myself back together. And to tell you the truth, I think I did a pretty good job."

Kent nodded, seeming to understand what she meant.

"Then, after all the work I had done to build a beautiful life for Peter, you decided that you could just show up again. So yes, I panicked."

"What did you think was going to happen?"

"I told you. I was scared that you would take Peter from me."

"So you decided you could just take him away from *me?*"

"I was protecting him."

"You were protecting yourself."

"Don't forget how we got here, Kent. If you hadn't taken off, none of this would have happened."

"You're blaming this on me? Look where we are, Lisa! I'm standing over my son's grave. You made me think he was..." He trailed off. Tears pooled in his eyes. "You made me think he was dead."

"It was the only thing I could think to do." She reached for his hand and whispered, "I'm sorry."

He pulled away before she could reach him. "Make no mistake of it. We're not here because of me." He looked her dead in the eye. "This is on you."

His words knocked the wind out of her. She tried to form a response, but she couldn't get anything out. He turned on his heel and walked back to his truck.

It took everything in her to keep her composure until he pulled out of the cemetery. It wasn't until the sound of his engine faded away completely that she sank to the ground and sobbed.

## 12

K ent thought back to the night he left Lisa...

The air of the warm summer night blew through the windows of the living room. Kent's face glistened with sweat from the humidity. It was one in the morning and he and Lisa had been fighting since he had come home from work five hours before.

"I can't live like this anymore, Kent." She threw her arms in the air and stood up from the couch, beginning to pace the living room floor. "You're hardly here, and I'm going crazy being with the babies every day. I need adult time, and date nights."

"You know we need the money. We both agreed that I needed to pick up some extra shifts."

She went on as if she hadn't heard a word he'd said. "And the twins never see you. They need time with their dad."

"I know that, but I don't know what you want me to do."

"Well, you think on that, because *this*"—she gestured to the room, vaguely alluding to their home life—"isn't working."

She walked to the hallway and returned carrying a fresh set of sheets, which she threw next to Kent on the couch. "And you can start that thinking right here on the couch tonight."

His head dropped down to his chest in defeat as she shut their bedroom door, and his shoulders slouched as he tiredly tucked the sheet into the couch cushions. With one pillow under his head and the other hugged to his chest, he stared at the heavily textured ceiling.

Chirps of crickets filled his ears. He tried to shut his eyes and let sleep take over, but the longer he lay there, the more awake he became. He had no idea what he could do to make things better. He and Lisa kept having the same argument over and over. She had asked him to work more so they could have more money, but now that he was working more, she was upset that he wasn't home very often. No matter what he did, she was upset with him.

After an hour of stewing, he decided to walk down the hallway to the twins' room. He tiptoed in and peeked over the edge to get a look at Andrew. The rhythm of his deep breathing was soothing. Sometimes he thought the only good thing to come of his and Lisa's marriage was the twins.

He crossed the room to Jeddie's crib and was startled when her brown eyes stared back into his. Without a stir, she gave him a smile, and Kent leaned down against the edge of the crib to brush her hair from her face. He wasn't there long before an idea crossed his mind. He tried to ignore the thought and looked deep into Jeddie's eyes, but it came back stronger. He shot straight up, leaving Jeddie in her crib, and went searching, as quietly as he could, around the house.

In the kitchen, he pulled baby food from the cupboards. He grabbed a laundry basket and filled it with his and

Jeddie's dirty clothes that were piled in the laundry room, then pulled the sheets and pillows off the couch.

He grabbed both his and Lisa's car keys and snuck into the garage. There he shoved his heavy load of clothes, linen, and food into his trunk. In the back seat of Lisa's car, he unhooked Jeddie's car seat, and installed it in the back seat of his.

With his heart pounding and sweat gathering around his collar, he paused in the kitchen, listening to make sure the house was still quiet. When he determined that Lisa was still asleep, he snuck back into the twins' room. The diaper bag hung on the closet door handle. He opened it and refilled it with diapers and wipes, and a few pairs of clean clothes for Jeddie.

He paused at Andrew's crib, wanting to remember everything about him, then gently bent down and gave him a kiss on the forehead. Backing away slowly, he made his way to Jeddie's crib and peeked over the edge again. He was once again surprised when she stared up at him. She smiled, this time with her whole body. He hesitated for just a moment, and then leaned down to pick her up.

"Hi, sweetheart," he whispered. "We're going to go for a ride, okay?"

Tiptoeing back to the garage, he remembered Lisa's car key in his front pocket, and set it on the counter before he closed the door behind him.

After buckling Jeddie in her seat, he got in his car and opened the garage door. He winced as the door and his car engine roared, and hoped that Lisa wouldn't wake until he was gone. When he was several blocks from the house, he finally turned on his headlights. Then, to hide his tracks as much as possible, he pulled in to the nearest gas station to fill up before he left town.

While waiting for the tank to fill, he pulled out his flip phone and turned it on silent. He told himself he was silencing his phone for Jeddie's sake so she could sleep on their drive, but in reality, he wanted to dodge Lisa's inevitable calls. He dropped it in the center console, then snapped the lid shut.

With no plan, Kent hit the highway heading north. He never intended to stay away for long, but the next morning had brought a new opportunity that changed his mind.

When he and Jeddie had woken up, he decided that despite driving all night, he didn't want to lounge in the hotel room all day. After feeding Jeddie, he buckled her in the car and started circling the small town's neighborhoods and retail areas.

"Can you believe this, Jeddie Bear?" he asked, pulling into a parking lot.

She smiled at him.

"Let's go find out who's selling this place."

Kent, with Jeddie in his arms, walked through the front gate and past the "For Sale" sign of a small plant nursery. It was on the edge of town. His mind was suddenly awash in daydreams about opening a nursery of his own.

He walked into the retail center and the smell of mulch and musty dirt hit him. He felt like he was home. In the corner, there was a middle-aged woman packing wind chimes into a box.

"Are you the owner of this place?"

"That's me." The woman looked up so that her brimmed hat no longer blocked her view of Kent.

"Can I ask why you're selling the place?"

"It's time. I'm getting too old for this stuff."

"How long have you owned it?"

"Thirty-five years."

"That's amazing."

"You interested? I could show you around."

"I would love that."

The woman spent an hour showing Kent the entire property. He grew more in love with every passing minute. Without thinking twice, at the end of the tour he was asking to buy the property.

"Honey, it's yours if you want it."

AFTER BUCKLING Jeddie into her car seat, he climbed into the driver's seat.

"I can't believe I just did that." He adjusted the mirror so he could see Jeddie in the reflection. "What do you think, sweetheart? You want to move to this town?"

She smiled back at him.

*Don't put her in the middle by pretending she wants this.*

Right then, he promised himself that he would never do that to his daughter again.

Just then, his phone started to ring, which made him regret turning the volume back on.

"Hello?"

On the other side of the phone, Lisa started to yell. "Where are you?!"

"I'm away. And I think it should stay this way for a while."

"Kent, you can't just take off in the middle of the night *with one of my kids* and never come back."

"Lisa, let's just take a step back for a minute, okay?"

"Take a step back from what?"

"I don't know, this situation. You and me. Everything. I think some space would be good for all of us."

"That is not something you get to decide on your own."

"Well, it's not something we are capable of deciding together. I can't even remember the last time you and I had a level-headed conversation."

She was silent.

"Look," Kent said. "I did what I thought was best in the moment. I am so tired of fighting. I don't want to fight anymore."

"I don't either."

"Okay. So let's take a break. Just temporary."

"What's temporary?"

"A few weeks? Maybe a month."

"A month?"

"We'll work it out. I'll keep in touch, okay?" He hung up the phone.

THEY WENT from talking every couple of days, to maybe once a month. From there, they both grew apart, ignoring each other's calls and doing their best to move on. Kent poured his energy into keeping his new business alive, and Lisa went back to nursing school.

Before either of them slowed down, seven years had passed and they each lived separate lives, never speaking anymore. It was their new normal, which both he and Lisa came to believe was for the best.

That was, until Jeddie turned eight.

That was the birthday all the questions started to come. Jeddie wanted to know every detail about her mother, and Kent decided it was best that he share nothing. He was unsure if they would ever see Lisa again, and he didn't want to risk Jeddie getting attached to the idea that she would be in Lisa's life someday. That possibility seemed unlikely to him.

There would have to be concrete evidence that they would be consistent in each other's lives before he would ever risk hurting Jeddie with false hope.

So, when Kent could no longer brush the subject of Lisa off easily, he made a phone call that would change everything. He dropped Jeddie off at school then pulled off the side of the road around the corner.

The phone rang several times before Lisa answered.

"Hello?"

"Hi, it's me."

"Kent?"

"Yeah."

"Is everything okay?"

"Yes."

"Oh. So, what's going on? Why are you calling?"

"I don't have the right to call you?"

"No, of course you do. It's just been a long time."

"Yeah, about that. I think it's time."

"Time for…?"

"Time for me and Jeddie to move back. I think the twins deserve to get to know one another."

"You want to move back?"

"Don't you think it's time?"

"I've thought that for a long time now," she said with an odd tone in her voice that Kent chalked up to nerves. "I just didn't know how you would take it."

"Really?"

"Yeah."

"That's wonderful."

"When are you thinking you'll move?"

"Oh, not for a couple of months. I would have to get ready to sell both the nursery and the house."

"So, this is happening? You're moving back?"

"Yes."

"That's really...great."

## 13

Lisa hung up the phone and paced the small supply closet at work where she'd taken the call.

*He can't come back.*

She stormed back and forth, thinking of how hard it had been to pick up and start over when Kent left.

*I am finally moving on, and he just thinks he can waltz back into our lives and disrupt everything? He's the one who left. He doesn't just get to decide when he's coming back.*

She needed to do something that would make it certain that Kent wouldn't take Peter away like he did Jeddie. Peter was the only good thing left in her life. If he was gone, she didn't know what she would do. There was also the slight problem that she had told Peter his dad had died. If Kent came back, Peter would know she'd lied to him. That lie was meant to keep Peter from searching for Kent. And the prospect of him coming back derailed what she viewed as a safety net.

While pacing, she remembered a news segment she had seen a week earlier about a house fire. She brushed it aside almost immediately, thinking how awful it was. But the image of the fire kept flashing in her mind. She couldn't help but think it could be an opportunity to take control of the situation.

AFTER WEEKS OF PLANNING, Lisa blew over her mug of hot cocoa as she sat at her kitchen table. Peter was roleplaying with his figurines in his bedroom. He was loud with excitement, as most eight-year-olds are. She moseyed to his bedroom to see what the noise was about.

Lisa propped her shoulder against the frame of eight-year-old Peter's bedroom door. He didn't notice her presence, and she delighted in a moment to watch her son undetected. Figurines lined the roof of the castle Peter had constructed out of Legos. She had given him the Legos the previous year for his birthday. Two days later, he had assembled trains, flowers, and cars. Lisa found herself in the toy store often, enthused by Peter's talent. She was curious to see what else he could build.

Tonight, Peter planned to crown a new king.

"Astronaut Harold, I hereby crown thee king. You are now the protector of this great kingdom. It is your responsibility to make sure everyone here stays safe." Peter took his play sword and rested it on his king's shoulder. Then, he raised it over the figurine's head to the opposite shoulder. Peter mocked the sound of trumpets and cheering of a crowd.

When the coronation was finished, he set King Harold by the door of his castle as a watchman for the night.

"Peter, it's time to go to Lakewood," Lisa announced.

"Do I have to go? I want to stay home and play. I promise I'll be really good."

"Sorry, sweetheart. I don't want you to be alone, and I have book club tonight."

Lisa brushed his hair off his forehead and kissed his cheek. "You'll have a great time like you always do."

After dropping him off at Lakewood, she rushed back home. She reversed into the driveway, making sure her car was ready for easy escape. Climbing into the attic, she set her plan in motion.

In the corner of the attic were stacks of boxes from her and Kent's life. They were things she had trouble parting with at the time Kent left—his and Jeddie's clothes, Jeddie's toys, memories from when she and Kent started dating, family pictures. She'd boxed everything and hid the boxes in the attic. She'd always been torn by two feelings: hope that Kent and Jeddie would return, and fear of the same thing. Now that the time for their return had come, fear had taken over.

She walked over and took the lid off the top box, revealing the last family picture of the four of them. She and Kent were holding each other tightly, and the twins were propped up in between them. Tears welled in her eyes as she looked at the family that seemed so foreign to her. So much had changed since that photo that she barely recognized herself.

Moments later, a baby picture of Jeddie caught her eye. Lisa was kissing her cheek in the photo and Jeddie's face was lit with a smile. Deciding she couldn't part with that one picture, she curled her fingers around it, holding onto it as she pulled herself away from the other pictures and put the lid back on the box. She knew that would be the last time she ever saw those memories and, in tears, she backed away with finality.

The exposed wire she had found a week before was

dangling from the attic wall. She walked over to it and held it in her hand. She thought through her plan one more time, mentally preparing herself for what she was about to do.

She thought about the morning after Kent had left. She had opened the door of the twins' room to only find Peter—or Andrew, back then. She had figured Kent was with Jeddie in the living room and went out to greet them. She will never forget the rush of panic that overcame her when she realized they were gone. She had felt like she'd been punched in the stomach, helpless.

Now, standing in her attic with the wire in hand, she felt those emotions as if it were that day. Determined to never let Kent make her feel that way again, she scraped the single match she brought with her against the wall and sparked a fire.

Then she ran.

Her shoes pounded against the wooden stairs, racing down them as fast as she could, shutting the door behind her.

Knowing she had to hide all evidence of foul play, she went to the sink in her mudroom and ran the match under cold water before shoving it to the bottom of her purse along with the picture of Jeddie. Then, looking in the mirror by the garage door, she calmed herself, freshened her lipstick, and walked, poised, to her car.

With a rev of her engine, she pulled out and drove to the next street over for book club.

"Lisa," Emily greeted. "How are you?"

"Doing great."

Most of the club members had already chosen their seats, and were gabbing while they waited for the rest of the members to show. She stayed calm, quietly taking a seat in the corner of the room. She held her copy of *The Catcher in the Rye* and shuffled through the pages.

*Just act normal and everything will be okay,* she thought to herself.

"All right, does everyone have their book?"

*You got this,* she tried to convince herself.

A heated discussion started among the group.

"Yes, but even though Holden had just gotten kicked out of school, there is no reason for his behavior!" one lady yelled.

"He was a boy who just got expelled and didn't want to face his family. It's Holden's coming of age story. Without him going off on his own, there would be no story," another lady chimed in.

"Well, there really wasn't a story anyway. I mean, come on. A boy goes off on his own into the city, tells us all these personal stories, and then says, 'You know what? I'm sick of telling my story so let's just end the book here.' Are you kidding me? It was a waste!"

Just then Carrie, another member of the book club, ran into the house, the door hitting and denting the wall in her haste to throw it open. She looked terrified. The conversation halted and everyone turned to look at her. She blurted, "Lisa, your house is on fire!"

"No," Lisa exhaled. She looked at Carrie. "Peter is at home asleep," she lied.

Without another word, Lisa was gone as the ladies collectively got up to go see the commotion.

Carrie, who had followed Lisa out the door, screamed after her. "Lisa!"

But she had already started her engine and pulled away from Emily's house.

*Sorry, Carrie,* she thought. *If anyone is going to believe me, I need to do this.*

Lisa was in full force, her right foot pressing hard on the gas pedal. Carrie hurried and got in her car to follow her.

When she pulled onto her street, the blaze of the fire caught her off guard. With all the plans she had made, she didn't stop to contemplate how hard it would be to see her home on fire. Tears welled in her eyes and spilled down her cheeks. *What have I done?*

Before she could rethink her choices, the reflection of Carrie's car zooming toward her pulled her out of her trance. Lisa flung the door open and ran toward her house. The raging heat of the fire hit her face and she threw her hand up to try and block it. When she got to the tapeline, two officers held up their hands and stopped her from crossing.

"Ma'am, you can't go any further," one of the officers said. His hair shined in the firelight.

"My son is in the house. You have to get my son!" She wrestled against the police officers with no success. "Peter!"

*I can't believe you are doing this,* she thought. *This is crazy.*

The officers looked at each other, dumbfounded. "Your son is in the house?"

"Yes! GET HIM OUT!" She could barely hear herself over the rumbling fire. Tears dropped from her cheeks and evaporated as they hit the asphalt. "Peter!"

"Ma'am?" An officer tried to get her attention. Lisa stared at the front door, genuinely frightened. After all the planning, she hadn't been prepared for the real thing. "Ma'am?" the officer said again.

Lisa looked down at the hand on her shoulder and then into the eyes of its owner.

"I need you to come with me."

*Stay calm. It'll be okay.*

The officer led her across the street.

"Now, I need you to tell me what you did tonight," the officer said.

*You knew this would happen. Just give him the bare minimum.*

"I fed Peter around six. He showered and then played with his Legos in his room until eight. I tucked him in, and then left for book club." Her voice cracked. "I was there for about thirty minutes, and then a friend of mine ran into the house to let me know my house was on fire. That's when I rushed over here."

She turned to see her now-blackening home. Shattered glass covered the lawn, crunching underneath the boots of firefighters. She closed her eyes to get some relief from the sting of the smoke.

After the officer took her statement, he had an EMT accompany her to the back of an ambulance. As she watched her front door for what seemed like hours, she could feel her eyelashes singeing and her face become tight. She rubbed her cheeks, softly attempting to regain motion, but her hands against her raw skin only felt more aggravating.

On the back bumper of the ambulance, she had a clear view of her home which she rarely broke focus from. An EMT checked her vitals every so often to make sure she wasn't in shock. She did everything she could to stay alert, to be ready for more questioning.

Smoke billowed from the roof like a blanket of clouds and nestled in the street below. Sirens filled the air as more personnel responded to the fire. Lisa watched a firefighter wrestle with the hydrant to attach his hose. Swarms of yellow-uniformed men blended against the hot orange blaze.

Realizing she was wrapped in a blanket, she pulled the corners in tight. Across the yard, she spotted two detectives talking to officers. Curious, she tried to hear them and leaned forward to get even an inch closer. The red and blue blinking lights lit up the night sky and distracted her. She closed her eyes, but still couldn't pick up their voices.

Neighbors had started to gather on all sides of the tape-line. People looked in on her like a mouse in a cage. Her gaze left the detectives and landed on the book club ladies, all huddled in a clump. Lisa wished she could hear them too. She could only imagine what gossip would spread from their mustering. But then again, she purposefully started the fire on a book club night in hopes that they would spread the news for her.

Hoses were strung across the yard, water flowing from them at full pressure. Lisa let her blanket drop and walked to the side of a fire truck directly in front of her house. Fire seeped out of the upstairs windows and fled to the roof. Her entire garage was roaring in flames. Where firefighters aimed their hoses, black smoke replaced the flames, but the flames returned as soon as they aimed their hoses to a different area. Then, with a loud crash, the roof over her garage collapsed.

She gulped with horror. "Peter," she whispered.

She ran toward the house, knowing officers would stop her. *It's the only way to make them believe me.*

"Let me go!" she cried, dropping to the ground and sobbing. She could barely catch her breath in the oxygen-deprived air. Her lungs closed off and she gasped for air.

A couple of officers pulled her off the ground.

"We need to get you across the street, ma'am. It's not safe here."

She let them lead her back to the ambulance where a team gathered to assess her situation.

She hugged her knees to her chest as they huddled around her. She could hear them mumbling about what to do with her as if she were nowhere near. As they discussed taking her to the police station, Lisa spoke up.

"I'm not going to the station."

"But ma'am—"

"My name is Lisa."

"Okay, Lisa. You would be much more comfortable at the station."

"Don't tell me how I would feel. Has your child ever been in a house fire before?"

"No, but—"

"No." Lisa waved her hand. "My son is in that house. I have been waiting here for hours and none of you have been kind enough to keep me informed." Her voice became louder, more desperate. "Where is my son?"

Her question hung heavy in the circle. Her focus shifted to a firefighter who had just come out of the front door and approached his captain. His stance was solemn as he informed the captain of what was behind the blackened brick wall.

The officer in the circle had followed her gaze and saw the same thing. He looked back at her, wrapping the blanket around her again. As she took hold of the corners, she said, "He's dead, isn't he?"

"I don't know for certain." His head was bowed.

"I do," she wept.

The officer looked up.

Lisa continued, weeping, "I knew the second that roof

came crashing down. I wanted so badly for him to be okay, but my baby is dead, and it's my fault."

"I am so sorry." The officer rested his hand on her shoulder.

Now, all these years later, Lisa sat on Peter's empty bed at Lakewood, having lost him anyway despite all of her efforts. She ran her fingers over the red stitches of the baseball Peter had left behind. The poster of Lou Gehrig mocked her as she stared at him. Her first lie to Peter about Kent being dead had led her to where she is now, alone.

Margie, who was walking past the bedroom door, had spotted her on the bed and poked her head into the room.

"Lisa? Are you all right?"

Margie waited at the door for Lisa to respond, but she just kept staring at the poster on the wall. When tears started to fall down her cheeks, Margie rushed to sit beside her. "Oh, hon." She put her arm around Lisa, rubbing her arm.

"This is all my fault," Lisa said through her tears. "What have I done, Margie?" She laid her head on Margie's shoulder.

Margie let her cry. She didn't know what to think of Lisa. Before Social Services arrived, Lisa seemed hardened and untrustworthy. Now that her outer shell had been cracked, she seemed weak and vulnerable. It was a side of her Margie had never seen before.

"Well, we're not going to solve anything by sitting around here." Margie stood up from the bed and walked over to the window. "Let's let the sunshine in." Margie pulled back the curtains and looked out onto the grounds.

She spotted a girl with dark brown hair walking around taking pictures. "Lisa, do you know who that is?" she asked pointing out the window.

Lisa walked over to join her. When she spotted who Margie was asking about, she breathed, "Jeddie."

PREPARING for the spring season at the nursery always required long nights of work. After Kent sent the staff home, he and Jeddie would often stay and put in another hour. It was Jeddie's busiest time of the year, not only with helping her dad, but with end-of-school projects, student council responsibilities, and track meets. Jeddie hardly had time for herself. But maybe that was the reason she piled on the loads of work. This time of year was especially hard for her with Mother's Day approaching, and with her mind occupied with everything else, she didn't have time to dwell on her mom.

Kent and Jeddie sat in his office going over their plans for a truckload of plants they were expecting in the morning. Kent had made a map of where he wanted everything to go, so when the truckload arrived it could be unloaded and organized efficiently. When they had just about finished and were packing up for the night, a woman barged into his office.

"What were you thinking, Kent?" the woman said.

Thrown off guard, Kent looked bewildered at the woman. "Lisa? What are you doing here?"

"Don't act like you don't know. You sent Jeddie to spy on me at Lakewood."

Jeddie stayed silent in the corner of the room; the

woman evidently hadn't spotted her yet. And Jeddie hadn't told Kent about either of her ventures to Lakewood.

Before Kent could rebut, Lisa went on. "If you wanted to know something, you should have just called me. Don't send your daughter to do your dirty work for you."

*Your daughter*, Jeddie thought. *So I'm nothing to you?*

"I would never do that." Kent stayed calm.

"I have enough going on right now, I don't need *her* poking her head around."

Lisa's words made all the nerve endings in Jeddie's face fire. She had never felt so belittled. Tears pooled in her eyes, and she looked at her dad for defense.

"Look, I don't know what happened, but I assure you, Jeddie wasn't there to spy on you. Maybe if you knew her you would understand that, but you *chose* to cut her out!"

"I had no other choice!"

Kent lost his cool and threw his hands in the air. "Ugh! Are you kidding me? I can't keep going in this circle anymore, Lisa! The only reason we are even in this situation right now is because you have never taken responsibility for your actions."

Jeddie's eyes widened in surprise. She had never seen her dad so upset.

"No, the reason we are in this situation is because I had to pick up the pieces when you left," Lisa argued.

Silence loomed in the room and Jeddie looked back and forth between her parents. Lisa still hadn't noticed she was in the room, and Jeddie was grateful for that.

Kent bit his lip, apparently deciding his next words carefully. "I tried to make amends." His voice was level. "I wanted to be a family again. And you...you were the one that made that impossible."

Kent's words triggered a memory for Jeddie. On her seventh birthday, Kent had invited all of the neighbors from their block, people she knew and loved. While she looked around the circle with bright smiling faces excited to sing to her and watch her blow out the candles, her mind slipped to her mom, the one person she wanted there. And with that, she had crinkled her eyelids shut, puffed her cheeks, and wished that she could meet her. The wish felt so sincere, that she believed, just for a second, that when she opened her eyes, her mom would be there. A stranger she had never seen would become the woman she most depended on. But when she opened her eyes one by one, the circle was filled with all the people she already knew. They clapped their hands and shouted cheers of celebration, and Jeddie bottled her wish and clapped with them.

As she thought back to that wish, she stared at Lisa, now right in front of her. The woman she had fought so hard for wouldn't even claim her as her daughter. All the restless nights daydreaming about meeting her mom, all the times she begged her dad, all the times she blamed him, were clouded by the woman she had fantasized her mother to be.

"You crushed me the night you left, Kent. I didn't see a way we could just pick up the pieces and start where we left off."

"One day at a time. That's all I wanted."

"I wasn't ready for that."

"So I've realized." Kent shook his head.

Lisa looked at him like she didn't know what to say.

"I think you'd better go," Kent said.

Obviously upset, Lisa turned on her heel to leave, only to stop when she spotted Jeddie. Showing no emotion, Jeddie stared at her as she stared back. For a moment, Lisa seemed apologetic, but without another word, she stormed out of the office.

## 14

In the morning, Jeddie saw Kent from the kitchen window sitting up in the tree house. After Lisa's visit the night before, Kent was very quiet about the whole thing. Jeddie wondered what he was doing now, sitting up in the tree house, but given the fact that he told her he needed some time, she decided to give him some space. For a bit. Thirty minutes to be exact, and then she couldn't take it anymore. She went out the back door and onto the patio, pausing for a minute before she approached the bottom of the stairs leading to the tree house and started to climb.

"Hey, kiddo," Kent greeted her.

"Dad?"

"Sorry, I just needed some space."

"I get that, but I think it might be better if we talked about this."

He bit his lip. "You're probably right."

"So...that was my mom last night..." She looked up to him for explanation.

"That was Lisa."

"You've been talking to her?"

"No, not talking, we talked...argued."

"She's Peter's mom too, isn't she?"

"Yes."

Jeddie paused for a minute before asking, "Then that means Peter is my brother?"

"More than just your brother...You and Peter are twins."

"Twins?"

"I know. I should have told you, but I just couldn't bring myself to do that." Kent looked down at Jeddie, who so desperately wanted him to go on. "When I saw that picture of...Peter and Lisa, I didn't know what to do. All these years, I thought he was dead."

"Wait...why?"

"Because that's what Lisa told me," Kent said, still in disbelief. "I don't know that I would have put everything together so quickly if you hadn't told me you visited Peter's burned-down home."

Jeddie looked at him, confused. When Kent saw the look on her face, he explained. "She had told me Peter died in a house fire."

"Why would she do that?"

"Your guess is as good as mine, but from her standpoint, I think she thought she was protecting Peter."

"She's the reason we moved here, isn't she?" Jeddie asked.

"At first, yeah. But then I saw this land, and I couldn't pass it up."

"So she has been in the town next to us this whole time?" Tears welled in her eyes.

Kent took a breath, and Jeddie could already feel the enormity of the truth that was coming. "Yeah...She really thought she was doing the right thing."

"By what? Faking Peter's death, or choosing to cut me out of her life?"

Kent looked at her, and Jeddie let her eyes plead him to tell her everything.

DIVULGING the truth about Lisa to Jeddie was easy except when it came to one part: his visit to Lakewood when she was twelve. That visit was the main reason Kent had decided he was never going to tell Jeddie about her mom, no matter how much she begged him. That visit broke his heart.

In the parking lot of Lakewood, he was practically begging Lisa to be a part of Jeddie's life. He had brought a picture of her to show Lisa so she could see what Jeddie looked like. Lisa had outright rejected getting to know Jeddie, and he *never* wanted Jeddie to know that.

But now, everything was happening so fast, and with Lisa's visit to the nursery the night before, there was no way he could keep the truth from Jeddie now.

"Your mom loves you, I know she does, even if she wasn't around."

"The fact that she never came around proves that she doesn't."

"I really think she was just...preoccupied."

"Did you even hear her last night? She wouldn't even call me *her daughter*."

Both of them dangled their feet off the edge of the tree house. Cricket chirps filled the warm spring air.

"I don't know, Jed. It's hard to understand, but she thought she was doing the right thing."

"Why do you keep defending her? Maybe when I was

younger it was good to keep me in the dark, but I look at that woman and all I see is manipulation and weakness."

"Jeddie..."

"No, you don't get to treat me like an imbecile anymore. She took everything away from you. She took everything away from *me*. I'm not just going to sit by and watch you defend her like what she did was okay."

"I never said you were an imbecile."

"Then why are you sitting here acting like she is so much better than you?"

"Because I'm the one who left!" His words were sharp, hitting the air between them.

Jeddie looked at him in disbelief, her eyes wide.

"And maybe she's right. Yeah, she may have gone over-board. But *I* left."

Kent watched the conflicting emotions flit across Jeddie's face before she said, "Well, you better figure out what you want, because the woman that barged into the nursery last night made it clear that she wants nothing to do with me."

Before Kent could process what Jeddie had said, she was stomping down the stairs. "Jeddie!" he yelled after her, trying to get her to stop. But she stepped inside and slammed the sliding glass door.

*What am I supposed to do?*

KENT WAS restless thinking back to everything that led to where they were. Now with all the lies out in the open, he stewed over everything Lisa had done. And as much as he tried to keep a level head about everything, he had to admit Jeddie was right. He shouldn't be defending Lisa, no matter how much he wished what she had done wasn't true.

The day Lisa had called him to tell him about Peter's death, everything changed in an instant. Just weeks before that, he had been hoping he and Jeddie would move back to town, and they could slowly work on being a family again. Even if that just meant for the kids to get to know one another.

Lisa had made it seem like she wanted him to move back, and that encouraged him. He really thought things would be better between them.

The day of the phone call, Kent's nursery was crowded with customers.

"Hello?" Kent answered. The garble of people talking in the background made it difficult to hear.

"Hi, it's Lisa."

"What?" His voice was raised.

"It's Lisa," she said, louder. "Could you find someplace quieter?"

"I'm a bit busy here," he breathed. "One sec." The noise faded as Kent relocated. He found his way through the sea of customers and shut himself in a storage room full of bags of mulch. "Okay. What's up?"

"I guess there is no easy way to say this…"

"Uh huh?" he said impatiently.

"There was a fire at my house last night."

Suddenly alert, he asked, "Is everything okay?"

"Well…"

"How is Andrew?"

"That's actually what I'm calling about," she said, her voice breaking.

"Is he hurt?"

He could hear her crying and listened intently.

"He…he didn't make it."

Kent repeated what she'd said. "He didn't make it. What

does that mean?"

"Kent...Andrew is dead."

The storage room filled with palpitating silence.

"I'm so sorry, Kent. There was nothing I could do."

The silence remained on his side of the phone.

"I'm going to plan a funeral. Just a small service. Just me...and you, if you want. I was thinking this Thursday."

The silence loomed, and for a minute she must have wondered if he was still on the phone. "Kent?"

Kent waited for a few seconds. "I'll see you on Thursday," he said, then hung up the phone. He had dreamed for a long time to finally be in his son's life again, and she had taken that hope away.

RECENT EVENTS also had Lisa up at night, reliving the past. Looking back at the desperate measures she'd taken to hide Peter made her feel sick inside. The morning of Peter's funeral service, Lisa pulled the mirror of her car down and looked into her own eyes. She was disappointed in what she saw. It wasn't the black circles under her eyes or the wrinkles; she had lost the glimmer. Looking in those eyes, she didn't recognize them. It only took a couple of days, but she had lost herself, and going forward with the next step of a funeral service meant she may never get the glimmer back.

Kent was already at the cemetery when she pulled in. Both of his hands rested on the casket. His head was bowed, and Lisa gave him a moment as it looked as though he were praying.

"Hey," she said when she got closer.

He didn't turn around. "Hey."

Lisa looked out across the cemetery. "Where's Jeddie? Did you bring her?"

"No."

"Oh. I was under the impression she would be here. Don't you think she would want to say goodbye to her brother?"

"Lisa, Jeddie hasn't seen Andrew since they were babies. She doesn't even remember him. I don't think it would be the best idea to give her a brother and then take him away in the same day."

"You don't talk about Andrew with her?"

"Are you telling me you talked to Andrew about Jeddie?"

"Well, no," she admitted.

"There you go then."

"Kent, can we just both be here for each other? Today is going to be hard enough." She felt her insides squirm.

He took a deep breath and crouched down. "I can't believe he's gone."

Lisa knelt down next to him, rested her head on his shoulder, and then she wrapped her arms around him. "I know. It's hard to process. Yesterday I wanted to tell him something, and I turned around, expecting him to be there."

*I am a horrible person,* she thought.

It was a subconscious act for both of them to hold on to each other. When they heard the officiator step to the head of the casket, they simultaneously broke off and stood.

The service was intimate, just as Lisa wanted. Although the entire town knew about Peter's death, Lisa purposefully left out the time of the service from his obituary. She had given the officiator some information for the eulogy, careful to only give him the name of Andrew. With every line said, Lisa wanted to take it all back, to tell Kent she was lying, but instead, she entwined her arm in his, took hold of his hand, and laid her head on his shoulder.

When the eulogy concluded, Kent took a step toward the casket to say a few words. "Although I haven't been physically near Andrew, I've always carried a part of him with me. You may think that I don't love him, but I do very much, Lisa.

"After we had that awful fight, I knew that it was time to leave...I loved you so much, but our marriage wasn't functioning. And because we were so young, neither of us knew how to communicate very well. The only thing harder than choosing to leave that night was choosing which kid to take with me. I took Jeddie because she was awake. Andrew was still sleeping and I thought if I took Jeddie, he wouldn't have to watch me leave.

"I don't regret taking Jeddie, but every day since, I have deeply missed my boy." Kent paused as tears pooled in his eyes. He knelt down next to the casket, kissed his hand then rested it on the casket's lid. "Goodbye, Andrew. Daddy loves you."

The service closed with the two of them, one after the other, placing a white rose on the black casket, and then watching as the casket was lowered into the ground. Kent and Lisa sat for hours in the reserved chairs under the green tent. They held each other's hand, and again, Lisa rested her head on his shoulder.

When the sun started to set, Kent looked down at his watch. He broke his grip on Lisa's hand as he stood. "I'd better go."

"So that's it?" With how much love she felt for him that morning, she didn't know what else to say.

"What's it?"

"You leave and I never get to see you or Jeddie again?"

she muttered. "We don't have to tell her about Andrew and take a brother away, but maybe you can give her a mother."

"I don't know, Lisa."

"Please?" she pleaded.

He started to walk toward his car then turned around. "Why don't you call me tomorrow and we can talk about it."

That was enough to let him go. She didn't intend to become involved in Jeddie's life, but at that moment, she needed hope that he really believed Peter was dead and that she wanted to be a family again.

AFTER TALKING to Jeddie in the tree house, Kent thought a lot about what he should do. Lisa showing up at the nursery the other night reminded him of why he kept Jeddie out of her life. Nothing had ever been simple with Lisa. And though she had been adamant about not getting to know Jeddie in the past, he was hoping, for Jeddie's sake, that Lisa would change her mind.

A few days later, Kent texted Lisa to see if they could meet up.

She responded with a place and time: "Ted's. 2:00 p.m." She and Kent used to eat at Ted's when they were dating.

Kent arrived at the diner ten minutes early to make sure he didn't miss her. He chose a table by the window so he could watch people as they passed.

A glimpse of Lisa in her red dress and jean jacket as she made her way down the sidewalk made him smile. It was small instances like this that made him remember why he fell in love with her in the first place.

She spotted him through the window and they each

waved. Kent stood when she came inside, and she walked over and gave him a hug.

"It's good to see you," he said.

"That's not how I'd imagined you'd greet me."

They pulled back, but he held on to her shoulders and looked directly in her eyes. "I'm kind of surprised myself," he said genuinely.

She gave him a small pat on the back. "Shall we?"

They sat down and opened their menus. Kent peered over the top of his, smiling at her short, blonde hair and red lipstick. She looked just as he remembered, except now she wore reading glasses so she could read the menu. She bit her lip as she decided what to order.

She looked into his dark eyes, and for a moment, it felt like they were twenty again. He grabbed her hand and held it in both of his.

"Lisa, I want you to know how—"

"So, how's the nursery?" Lisa pulled her hand from his, picking up her menu again.

He cleared his throat, feeling awkward about her sudden interruption. "It's really good. I wish you would come by and see it...I mean officially. Not like the other night."

"I've driven by a few times, but never made it in there."

"What? Why didn't you tell me?"

"I don't know. Just afraid, I guess."

"Afraid of what?"

She ignored the question, and instead asked her own. "So, you wanted to talk?"

"Uh...yeah. I just wanted to see how you were doing?"

"That's it?"

"Well, that, and I came to talk about Jeddie."

"Oh." She sunk back in her seat.

"Come on, Lisa. I think it's time for you two to get to know one another."

"I don't think that's a good idea."

"Why are you avoiding this? I don't get what is keeping you from wanting a relationship with your daughter."

"You wouldn't understand."

"She seems to think you made it pretty clear that you don't want a relationship with her."

"Because she shouldn't want to get to know me."

"Did you say something to her at Lakewood?"

"I didn't say *anything*," she scoffed. "I was shocked to see her. The first time she was there I was getting in my car, and she was standing there, staring at me."

"She's just a kid, Lisa. She wants a mother."

"Well, that's one thing I don't think I can give her."

"That's the one thing she deserves the most."

"Exactly. And she's practically an adult. I don't have anything to offer her."

"You crushed her."

"Listen, I'm not the one who took off in the middle of the night."

"Don't bring that up again. I am so tired of you pinning this situation on me."

"I didn't even get to say goodbye to Jeddie."

"She was right there in front of you at Lakewood. Why didn't you take a chance?"

"As much as I want to, Kent, I really think it would just be better if I stayed away."

"Please don't do this." He leaned in closer to her.

"I'm sorry, Kent. I really do wish you and Jeddie all the best." She got up and tossed her menu on the table before walking out the door.

"Dad, you here?" Jeddie asked as she walked in the back door of his office.

"In the washroom."

"What are you doing?" The place was a mess.

"Just some spring cleaning."

She let out a chuckle. "So this is how you deal with stress?"

"I just needed to occupy my mind."

"Did something happen today?"

"No."

Jeddie eyed him. He wasn't his normal cheery self. Then she remembered the conversation they'd had a few days earlier. "Listen, I'm really sorry about the other night."

"I know."

"Then why do you seem upset?"

"Just a little frustrated. But not at you."

"What happened?"

"I don't think it's a good idea for me to tell you."

"You talked to her, didn't you?"

Kent sighed. "She and I met at Ted's."

"And?"

"And it was disappointing, like it always is."

"It couldn't have been that bad."

Kent gave her a look that said it was.

Jeddie lent a hand in cleaning up. "I've been thinking too."

"Yeah?"

"Do you remember what Peter told us about his dad?"

"It's crossed my mind," he said as he knelt down and stuck his head in a cupboard. He started pulling everything out and spreading it across the floor.

"Dad, Peter said his dad died from Lou Gehrig's disease. That means Lisa lied about you being dead too."

"I know."

"So, what, she just lied to both of you so neither of you would go looking? And she didn't lie about me because Peter doesn't even know he has a sister."

"Yeah. I'm not sure how to break the news to him."

"I don't think she meant to hurt him, Dad."

"So now you're defending her?"

"Not really defending. Just trying to understand."

"When did you get to be so grown up?"

"About two days ago," she said, smirking. "Dad, the other night at the nursery, she seemed more ashamed than anything. Maybe she's stayed away so she can keep what little pride she has left."

"Maybe. But that's not really an excuse." He pulled out a box of files and carried it to his desk. "We've all done things we're not proud of."

"It seems like both of you made drastic decisions in a moment of desperation."

"Are you my therapist now?"

"Do you want me to be?"

"Jeddie..."

"Come on, Dad. I may not ever understand it, but then again, I don't know the woman. But like I said, it sounds like both of you made desperate decisions in the hopes you were doing the right thing. And maybe you did the right thing then. But now...now might be the right time for all of us to move forward."

～

MARGIE WAS at her desk when she saw fifteen-year-old Peter sneaking down the hallway. As he got older, he'd memorized his mom's schedule and knew when he would remain unseen by her. From everything Margie had observed, Lisa had lost her maternal love for Peter. And though she had to lie to Lisa, she welcomed Peter's visits. She felt she was doing what was best.

Margie always had a weird feeling about Lisa and Peter living at Lakewood, like something wasn't quite right. When they had first arrived, their administrator had sent out a memo to all employees explaining that Peter and Lisa would be residing at Lakewood, and no questions were to be asked. Margie had ignored that last part.

"Lisa, I'm worried about you and Peter. Is everything all right?" She had pulled Lisa aside one day and asked her privately.

"Everything's fine," she answered pointedly.

"Are you sure? It just seems a little weird that you would choose to live here of all places."

"Well, I didn't *choose* to live here. I didn't really have a choice."

"What do you mean?"

"My house burned to the ground."

"Oh no...I am so sorry."

"Don't be sorry. Things happen." Her answer was matter of fact.

"But that was your home."

"Margie, don't make this into a big deal. This is why I didn't want questions. And while we're on that subject, you have to promise me you won't tell Peter."

"Tell Peter what?"

"That our home burned down."

"You mean he doesn't know?"

"No. He was here the night of the fire."

"That's pretty fortunate," Margie thought out loud.

"Yes, I am very grateful he was out of harm's way."

"Why don't you want him to know?"

"He was so attached to that home. I just think it would break his heart."

"Lisa..."

"Cheer up. And don't bring this up again," Lisa said, leaving the room before Margie could even think to reply.

It all just seemed odd. For losing her home, Lisa didn't seem upset at all. Then she wanted to keep it a secret from Peter. And on top of that, she kept him locked in their room almost every day. The puzzle had never quite fit in Margie's mind.

Peter's visit today put her over the edge.

He sat slouched in the chair next to her at the nurses' station, swiveling back and forth.

"What's up, kid?" Margie asked.

"Nothing. Nothing is ever up."

"Did you get to play games with the patients today?"

"The same games. Over and over and over."

"Have you talked to your mom about it?"

"Not lately. It's not worth it. She won't hear what I'm saying."

"I'm sorry."

"I just don't understand why we're living here. Why can't we just go back to our house? Why can't I go back to a normal school? Why can't my mom go back to being who she was before we came here?"

All of his questions had her mind turning. *Maybe there never was a fire.* It occurred to her that she had never done anything to confirm Lisa's story. She had never felt the need to until now. She was so busy trying to be a supportive friend, it never crossed her mind that Lisa might have made the whole thing up. When Peter was back in his room, Margie pulled up her search engine and looked for house fires that happened seven years ago in their county. It took about thirty minutes before she came across the article.

She stared and stared at the title, not believing what she was reading.

### Eight-Year-Old Boy Dies in House Fire

The article was dated June 30 and if Margie's memory was serving her correctly, it was in the middle of the summer when Lisa and Peter started living at Lakewood. She continued reading in disbelief. Then she came across the line that didn't allow her to deny the truth.

*"Lisa Doyle, the mother of the young boy, stayed at the scene all night waiting for firefighters to carry her son out of the house, to no avail."*

Her heart beat fast as she printed out the article and shoved it in her purse. Without a word, she left the building and got into her car.

"She *faked* his death?" she asked herself. "Why in the world would she do that?"

Margie's mind was working so quickly now that she found herself calling her friend Angela, who worked for the Department of Children and Family Services.

"Hello?"

"Angela, its Margie. Can we meet? I need to talk to you in person."

"Sure. I was actually about to leave the office for lunch."

As they sat down to eat, Angela could tell something was bothering Margie.

"Sweetie, are you okay?"

"Angela"—Margie looked around to make sure no one was listening—"I just found something that I need you to look at."

She pulled the crinkled news article out of her purse and passed it to Angela, who started to read.

"This article is seven years old. What's so significant about it?"

"You know Lisa that I work with?"

"Yes."

"That article is about her."

"That is so sad. She lost her kid to this fire?"

"That's the thing." Margie's heart thumped in her chest. "That kid is still alive."

"What?" Angela looked back at the article.

Margie leaned in and lowered her voice. "He and Lisa have been living at Lakewood."

"So why does the article say he died?"

"I think Lisa faked his death. She has always been *so* weird about Peter, her son, living there. She is controlling and locks him in their room. She hides from him the fact that their house burned down. The whole situation is just strange."

Angela matched her whisper. "Why would she fake his death?"

"I don't know. But what I do know is that her kid hates living there. And really, it is no place for a kid to grow up. He deserves a normal life. I can't just stand by now and do nothing. Especially after finding this article."

"So why are you telling me?"

"Well, I thought that because you work for Social Services, maybe you could step in and do something."

"I don't know... This is not really the kind of case I would normally deal with."

"Angela, if Lisa faked Peter's death, don't you want to be part of the reason we find out why? Don't you want to give him a better life?"

"You know I want that for all kids."

Margie looked at her with pleading eyes until she agreed.

"All right, I can look into this and see if there is a way we can step in."

"Thank you."

"You bet."

"Can I just ask one more thing?"

"What?"

"Please don't let Lisa know that I'm the one who tipped you off."

"I'll see what I can do."

K ent tapped his thumb on the steering wheel of his car as Jeddie sat next to him in the passenger seat. It seemed they were both consumed by their own thoughts. Kent wound through the back roads to Elaine's house where they were headed to break the news to Peter.

Jeddie thought about all the information Kent had bombarded her with over the last few days. First, there was the fact that he took off with her when she was just a baby. Then there was Lisa burning her own house down. And she was still in shock about Peter being her twin. The more she thought about that last part, the more conflicted she became. She had heard that twins have some sort of intuition about each other, that they were connected, but it had never crossed her mind that she had a twin. Yes, she had always felt like there was a part of her missing, but she attributed that feeling to not knowing her mom. The fact that she had never figured out she had a twin made her feel like a fraud. She kept thinking that if she had known about

Peter, maybe she could have done something. Maybe she could have saved him from such an awful childhood.

Most of all, she was conflicted about her feelings toward Lisa. The woman she had idealized, the woman she had always dreamed of meeting, wasn't the person she had dreamed she'd be. Jeddie wanted to do what was best for Peter, but for her, when she was telling Kent it was time to move forward, she meant it was time for her to move on, without Lisa.

They pulled up to the front of Elaine's house and both of them just stared out of the windshield for a minute before getting out of the car.

"It'll be okay, Dad," Jeddie said reassuringly.

He wrapped his arm around her shoulder and, side by side, they walked to the front door.

Jeddie's heart pounded as Kent knocked on the door. *Would Peter accept them as his family?* Jeddie couldn't help but think, sure her dad was wondering the same thing.

When Elaine answered the door, Kent's face went white looking nauseated. Jeddie and Elaine quickly helped him inside, walking him over to one of the living room chairs.

Elaine filled a glass with water for him, and he gulped it down. The empty glass shook in his hand and Jeddie took it from him before it fell on the floor.

Elaine looked at Jeddie and mouthed, "Is he okay?"

Jeddie shrugged, but also shook her head. She knew he wasn't. Not only would he have to explain to Peter that he was his dad, and why his house had burned down, but he was going to have to explain to him why he took off in the middle of the night with Jeddie all those years ago.

"Is Peter here?" Jeddie asked.

"Yes, he'll be down in a minute."

As they waited, Jeddie's leg bobbed up and down. She

couldn't control her nerves, and by the looks of her dad, he hadn't been able to compose himself at all since they walked through the door. Conversations had always been easy with Elaine, but today was different. She spoke no words, but her looks back and forth between the two of them spoke loudly.

Without a word, she got up from her chair and walked over to the bottom of the stairs. "Peter? You coming?" Elaine called.

"Almost."

She looked back at Jeddie and Kent, and broke the awkward silence. "How is the nursery, Kent?"

Jeddie tapped her foot against his calf when he didn't answer.

"Huh?" he questioned, looking at her.

"Elaine asked you about the nursery," Jeddie explained.

He gave her a robotic answer. "It's good. This time of year is always busy."

"I'm sure. Getting ready for Mother's Day and vegetable season."

"That's right."

"And Jeddie, how is school?" Elaine asked, still looking worried at Kent.

"Good. The school year is almost over. Peter and I need to turn in our assignment, but I'm not sure that's such a good idea now."

"That's right. You two said you had something you needed to tell Peter?" she asked.

"Yep."

"I'm assuming after your exit the other day, Kent, that it has something to do with that picture right there?" She pointed to the picture of Peter and Lisa.

"That's when everything started to come to light, yes," Kent said.

Just then, Peter walked in and sat on the chair by Elaine.

"Hey, guys. Sorry about that."

"Hey." Jeddie's face lit up with a giant smile that she must have kept for a few moments too long.

"Are you okay?" Peter asked.

"Oh, yeah." Her smile faded in an instant.

"Elaine said you guys needed to talk to me. What's up?" It was the calmest Jeddie had ever seen Peter. He was almost confident. She wished she could pause and capture this moment because she knew that after what Kent was about to say, he would be anything but calm.

She nodded her head toward Peter while looking at Kent to let him know he was the one that needed to speak, and eventually, he did.

"Uh...Peter, you remember how I left your house pretty abruptly the other day?" Kent's gaze was bolted to the brown shag carpet.

"Yeah."

"I'm really sorry about that."

"It's okay. No need to be sorry."

"Actually, there is." Kent looked at Jeddie, who prodded him along. "I know the woman in that picture. Your mom. She and I have...a history together."

"What do you mean?"

"I mean that if she's your mom, then that means...I'm your...dad." His last word pierced each of their ears as it echoed in the silence. Kent's head still hung low as he shot a glance at Peter. Confusion settled on his face.

Elaine was the first one to speak up, saying what Peter was probably thinking. "But I thought Peter's dad was dead."

"I did too. Until I found out that *I* am his dad. So...not dead." He gave a nervous chuckle.

"How is this possible?" Elaine asked. She seemed more shocked than Peter.

Kent scooted to the edge of the couch. "Peter, I was married to your mom a long time ago. But things didn't work out and we ended up splitting. Over time, we had agreed we would each get half of everything we had, which also meant half of our kids."

Elaine seemed to catch on to what Kent was about to say. "So...does that mean that Jeddie...?"

"That Jeddie what?" Peter asked, his anger starting to seep through.

"I'm the other half of their kids, Peter."

"What?"

"You're my twin brother."

"No..."

"I know this is a lot to take in Peter, but it's the truth," Kent said.

"No. I don't believe you. My mom said my dad died. She wouldn't lie to me."

"She lied to you, just like she lied to me," Kent replied.

"What do you mean?"

"Peter, your mom led me to believe that you died in a house fire. But I've come to find out that your mom started that fire to fake your death. I attended your funeral...Well, your fake funeral."

"No. She wouldn't do that."

Jeddie tried to calm him. "Peter..."

"Why are you making this up?" Peter demanded.

"I wish we were."

"My mom didn't do this."

"Peter, I talked to her, and she admitted to it," Kent said simply.

He didn't respond, but instead got up and walked out the

kitchen door into the backyard. The three of them watched him go, then Elaine looked back at Kent.

"Are you sure about this, Kent? Is this really true?"

"I didn't want to believe Lisa would do something like this either, but I confronted her a few days ago and she confirmed it."

"Why did she do it?"

"Well, I'm still trying to understand her thinking. She told me that it all started when I took off with Jeddie in the middle of the night."

"Oh?"

"Dad, while you fill Elaine in, I'm going to go talk to Peter," Jeddie said.

She exited out the sliding glass door of the kitchen and found Peter sitting on the patio bench. He didn't acknowledge her when she sat down next to him.

"Hey."

He didn't answer.

"What are you thinking?"

He shook his head. "I'm thinking I don't know who to be mad at."

"I felt the same way a couple of days ago."

"Jeddie, why would my mom do this?"

"From everything my dad has told me, as crazy as it sounds, I think she was trying to protect you."

"From what?"

"My dad...I think she thought he would take you from her. Like he took me."

"But *fake* my death? That's insane!"

"I don't think she saw it that way."

"Why are you defending her?"

"Look, Peter, I am more upset with her than you can imagine. My whole life I had to deal with the fact that my mom *chose* not to be in my life. She didn't even want to give me a chance. And I don't know...Now that I know the whole story, I've been trying to see everything from her point of view."

"You don't know what it was like to live in that place."

"No, but I do know what it's like to find out you have a twin. Can we just be happy about that? I've always thought my brother died when I was little. Now that I know that's not true and that *you* are my brother...Well, it makes me hopeful for the future."

He nodded; that, at least, was something they agreed on.

"Good." She stood up from the table. "Now that that's settled, I'd like to introduce you to your dad, who, might I add, is really nervous. Please give him a chance, Peter." She held her hand out and they walked back in the house together.

"There you are," Elaine said.

Peter gave her a weak smile.

"Jeddie, would you mind helping me carry some things to the shed?" Elaine put her arm around Jeddie and guided her outside. Jeddie looked over her shoulder, wanting to stay. "I think it would be good to give the two of them a minute alone," Elaine explained.

BACK IN THE LIVING ROOM, Peter awkwardly took the chair Elaine had been sitting in. He stared at his hands until Kent finally spoke.

"Peter, I can only imagine how hard this must be for you. I just want you to know that I am really sorry."

Peter kept staring at his hands, silent.

"I wish I would have figured everything out sooner. It

just didn't click until I saw that picture of you and your mom."

With silence still on Peter's end, Kent kept going.

"I want you to know that me taking off with Jeddie in the middle of the night had nothing to do with you. I don't love her more. Even now. I have never stopped loving you, Peter."

"So why didn't you catch on sooner?"

"Well, for starters, I knew you as Andrew, not Peter."

"Andrew?"

"Yeah. Your mom must have changed your name when you were too little to remember."

"I just don't understand why she did this."

"I've known for a few days now, and I'm still having a hard time wrapping my brain around it."

"She made everyone think I was dead. That's why she kept me locked up at Lakewood all these years?"

"I know."

"And it's your fault that she did that?"

"Well, I'd like to think not." *What did Jeddie say to him?*

"You took off with Jeddie, so she thought you would do the same with me?"

"Maybe. But Peter, please understand. Your mom and I were so young when we had you two... And I just couldn't take the fighting anymore."

Peter went silent again.

"I really wanted you in my life, Peter. That's why I planned to move back here. But the chance to be a family was gone as soon as Lisa burned your house down. She had already told you I was dead, and there was no way she was going to become the bad parent who lied to her son. So, she covered up one lie with another, and came up with a plan that kept us apart."

"Did you say there was a funeral?"

"Yeah."

"So she really went all in." He rubbed his face with both hands.

"She sure did."

The air was thick between them. Only the sounds of an occasional house creak split through the air. Peter hadn't looked up once in the last five minutes. He looked to be in the middle of a mental debate with himself, and Kent didn't blame him.

"Look, Peter..." Kent said, breaking the silence. "I was where you are a few days ago. In fact, I was barely functioning. I was so engulfed in my own thoughts and seething with anger that I barely acknowledged people around me, even Jeddie...What I'm trying to say is, I know this is a lot to take in."

"I just need some time."

"I can give you that."

Kent realized that if he had any hope of a relationship with Peter, he would need to adhere to that promise. He would need to give him the time to process. He walked over and put his hand on Peter's shoulder, then went over and poked his head out the back door. "Jeddie, time to go."

"But Elaine and I are almost done," she said, loading a box of gardening tools into the shed.

"Come on," he said in a gentle voice.

With a solemn look, she walked back into the living room. With tears in her eyes, she walked over to Peter and gave him a hug. "Don't wait too long to reach out, okay?"

WITH PETER'S file spread over the kitchen counter, Elaine and Angela sat on the barstools. The two of them were going over what options were available. Now that they knew Kent was Peter's dad, it was Angela's opinion that the courts would most likely rule in Kent's favor for guardianship.

"What about Lisa?" Elaine asked.

"With everything that has come to light, including the house fire, she will most likely be facing felony charges for arson."

"Oh..." Elaine's cheeks turned red. She glimpsed out the kitchen window at Peter. He was sitting in the shade of a tree, reading a book.

"Kent is his dad. So it only seems natural that Peter be put in his care," Angela explained.

"I think so too. I'm just really going to miss having him around here."

"Well, I have no doubt that Kent and Jeddie will keep you close."

As the weekend approached, Jeddie didn't know how much longer she could take Kent's sulking. Still wanting to give Peter his space, she decided to text Elaine.

*Just reaching out to see if there are any updates on your end...*

Elaine responded, *Going over everything with Angela. Peter will reach out when he is ready.*

Elaine's response made Jeddie realize that she was feeling the same way her dad was. She was just hiding it better. Reluctant to leave the house, but wanting a distraction, she decided to attend the baseball game that night.

"Jeddie, over here!" Natalie yelled at her from the bleachers.

Jeddie approached her, forcing a smile.

"Where've you been lately? I feel like I haven't seen you all week."

"I wouldn't know where to begin..."

Natalie looked at her intently.

Jeddie looked back at her best friend, knowing she could confide in her. "Well...I met my mom this week."

"Wow. How did that go?"

"Let's just say I don't think we're going to go get mani-pedis any time soon."

"Oh, Jed. I'm so sorry."

"Me too. You know, I just thought it would be a lot better meeting her. But it turns out she wants nothing to do with me."

"I'm sorry.."

"There's something else..." Jeddie started.

"What?"

"Nat. If I tell you this, you have to promise to keep this to yourself."

"Promise."

Jeddie knew she was sincere. Natalie had never broken any of her promises to her.

"Peter is my twin brother."

Natalie was obviously thrown off guard. "Wait, what? How is that possible?"

"That's how everything came to light. My dad saw a picture of Peter and my mom, and figured everything out."

Just then Jeddie felt a tap on her shoulder. She turned to find Peter.

"Hey," he said. "Mind if I sit with you?"

Jeddie looked back and Natalie who must have sensed that they needed some space. "I'm gonna go grab a snack," Natalie said.

When Peter joined Jeddie on the bleachers, she asked, "So how are you doing?"

"I'm not sure, to be honest."

"That's okay. Nobody is expecting you to be okay."

"This is all just so much to take in. I feel like I'm barely functioning."

"I can't even imagine what's going through your head."

"Jeddie, what are we supposed to do now?"

"I think just take it day by day. That's all we can do."

Jeddie's sympathy ran deep for Peter, but her guilt consumed her. It had all been a lucky chance that she was the one Kent took off with. If she had been asleep and Peter awake, the situation could have easily been reversed. Looking at Peter, she wondered if he would ever be able to overcome his childhood at Lakewood, but with him coming to her tonight, it gave her hope that one day, he would. She would just have to be patient.

IT HAD BEEN a week since Kent had broken the news to Peter. With every passing day, Kent grew more nervous that Peter didn't care to get to know him. One morning, Jeddie eyed him from the table as he walked into the kitchen, eyes red and bloodshot, before completely forgetting why he'd gone in there in the first place. He walked back to his room and shut the door.

Suddenly, Kent's phone rang loudly on the kitchen counter and Kent swung open his bedroom door so fast it pelted into the wall. Sure enough, it was Peter's name that flashed on the home screen. Kent gave Jeddie a hopeful look, and she nodded to let him know it was the call he had been waiting for. He sprinted down the hallway, kicking up a breeze that made the family pictures sway side to side on their hooks. Jeddie thrust the phone toward him so he could answer.

"Hello?" His breathing was uneven.

"Hi, it's Peter."

"Hi," he said, trying not to sound too excited.

"I was wondering..."

"Yeah?" Kent looked at Jeddie, hopeful.

"Would you take me to the cemetery where my grave is?"

It certainly wasn't what Kent had expected, but at this point, he would do anything to spend time with him. "Sure. Could we pick you up in say...thirty minutes?"

"Yep. I'll be ready."

Kent set the phone on the counter and before either of them said a word, they ran to their bedrooms, racing to see who could get ready and to the car faster than the other. Although the situation was unexpected, both Jeddie and Kent were ready to move forward with life, as a family, with Peter. It seemed they were both hoping today would be the start of that new life.

Peter was waiting on the front porch with Angela when they pulled up to the house. Peter helped himself into the back seat, and Angela walked over to Jeddie's window, motioned for her to roll it down.

"We haven't been ordered to supervise your visits, but I trust you'll bring him back in one piece?"

"Of course," Kent said.

Angela backed away and waved them off.

"So, to the cemetery?" Kent asked.

"Yep," Peter confirmed.

"Any particular reason?"

"I just want to see it for myself."

"I kind of want to see it too," Jeddie said.

It was about a ten-minute drive to the cemetery. When they arrived, Kent got out of the car and guided Peter and Jeddie to Peter's fake headstone. They all looked at it, reading what it said, and just stood there in surprise.

Peter reached into his pocket and took out a Lego figurine.

"When I was little, my mom told me that you had died from Lou Gehrig's disease. After that, I became a bit of a baseball fanatic. I think it was my way of trying to connect with you. I found out everything I could about Lou Gehrig and baseball. I figured if I knew everything about Lou Gehrig, then I would somehow know my dad."

He held his Lego friend up so that Kent could see.

"When my mom bought me this guy with the baseball cap and jersey, I couldn't let him go. I named him Lou, and I've carried him around in my pocket every day since I've been at Lakewood."

"Peter, that means a lot to me, really," Kent said.

"I don't know what's going to happen now, but I was really hoping we could leave this in the past." He pointed to the headstone.

"We would both like that. We really want to be the family we were meant to be."

"I do too."

Tears rolled down Jeddie's cheeks as she smiled.

Peter took one last look at Lou, and as a gesture of leaving everything in the past, he set him on top of the headstone. Kent wrapped his arms around Peter and Jeddie. All three of them stared at Lou as he stared back at them. Peter patted his pocket where he had always kept Lou. Instead of an empty hole, he felt a weight lifted. Peter smiled, as tears welled in his eyes. Leaving Lou behind made him feel like he was finally free.

A COUPLE OF WEEKS LATER, Elaine sat on Peter's bed, watching him pack his things to move to Kent's home. "You can keep some of your things here. That way, you can come visit any time."

Peter, who was bagging up his clothes, paused and looked up at Elaine who looked as if she were about to cry. "Elaine?"

She wiped underneath her eyes. "I'm sorry, kiddo. I just didn't think this was going to be so hard."

"I know." He was struggling too, with the idea of leaving Elaine. If it weren't for her, he wouldn't have adjusted to leaving Lakewood as well as he did.

"You came into my life at the exact moment I needed it, Peter. And I just don't know what I'm going to do with myself now that you're leaving."

Peter felt a pit in his stomach. Elaine's mouth had sagged into a frown. "I'm so sorry, Elaine."

"Oh, Peter, I shouldn't be laying this burden on your shoulders. This is not your fault, and I know I'll be okay."

"We're all family now. I don't think you need to worry about being alone."

Elaine gave him a small smile. "You're a great kid, you know that?"

"It must be because I had a pretty great foster mom." He walked over and embraced her in a hug. "Thank you, Elaine. For everything."

ALL SEASON, Kent and Jeddie had been preparing for Mother's Day weekend. Now that it had arrived, they both scurried around the nursery making sure tables were filled with plants, hanging baskets were proudly displayed, and makeshift registers were rolled outside to accommodate the floods of customers they were expecting.

Before they opened the gates, the parking lot had already started to fill up.

Kent put his arm around Jeddie. "You ready to do this again?"

"Ready as I'll ever be."

They each took a side of the gate and swung it open, immediately greeting customers as they walked in.

The morning rush turned into an afternoon rush. In all the chaos, Jeddie finally found a minute to sneak to her dad's office to grab a drink and tie her hair back. As she walked out the back door, a woman in a baseball cap seemed to be waiting for her.

"Can I help you?" Jeddie asked.

The woman looked up so Jeddie could see her face beneath the cap. "Hi, Jeddie. Do you think we could talk for a minute?" It was Lisa.

Still brewing over their encounter in her dad's office a few days earlier, Jeddie wasn't sure if she wanted to talk to her. "I'm pretty busy."

Lisa gently grabbed Jeddie's arm. "I know I'm not your favorite person, but I just want you to understand."

"What's there to understand?" Jeddie said, fighting back tears.

"Jeddie, I always wanted you in my life. I need you to know that."

She could no longer suppress her emotions. "How could you possibly say that? You were in the next town most of my childhood and you made *no* effort."

"I didn't know how."

"You didn't even try. My dad told me he asked you several times to be in my life, and each time you rejected me."

"I was so caught up in keeping Peter a secret..." she trailed off before adding, "I was afraid if I turned my focus to you, something would slip."

"Can't you see how twisted your reality is? You and my dad made all of these decisions when Peter and I were young, and we're the ones paying for those decisions. You're not helping us."

"Please, Jeddie."

"No. Just do me a favor and stay away from me."

"Jeddie..."

Jeddie threw up her arms as she started to back away. "I'm just giving you exactly what you've asked for."

Lisa stepped toward her. "I guess I don't expect you to forgive me, but please, just take this letter."

Jeddie looked at the envelope in Lisa's hands with her name on it. She wanted more than anything to have the strength to walk away without giving her the satisfaction of taking it, but her curiosity took over. She let Lisa hand her the letter, then turned and walked down the gravel pathway to help another customer.

LISA'S EYES skimmed over the crowd, looking for Kent. When she spotted him, she walked over and hovered near him as he finished with a customer.

When he saw her, he quickly turned his attention back to the customer. "Yes, all of these shrubs right here are sun plants. Take a look around, and if you have any more questions, let me know." He walked away from the customer.

They both awkwardly approached each other. Kent stood with both hands in his pocket, which made Lisa feel like she couldn't hug him like she wanted to.

She cleared her throat. "It, uh...looks like I'll be going away for a little while..." Lisa said.

"They've decided to charge you?"

She reached for his hand, but he didn't reciprocate. "Now that the police know I started the fire, there's a chance I could go to prison."

"They told you that?"

"It's not definitive yet. My court appearance is set for next week, but I intend to plead guilty."

"If you're pleading guilty, couldn't they just do a settlement?" Kent asked.

"I don't want that."

"Why?"

Her cheeks reddened, she was trying to hold back the tears that were rapidly welling in her eyes. She didn't answer the question out loud for Kent, but all she could think is that prison seemed like the better option. Better than facing her family now that they know what she did.

She pleaded for forgiveness and he gave in. He took his hands out of his pockets and wrapped her in a warm embrace, and she fell into him. She looked back at Jeddie, who was watching the two of them while helping a customer. She looked unamused, holding her stance, her arms folded. Lisa gave her a small smile and a gentle wave. Then she pulled back from Kent and looked into his eyes, wiping her tears from his shoulder.

Raised on her toes, she kissed him on the cheek. Then she leaned to the side and whispered in his ear, "I'm sorry."

Kent's heart sunk deep in his chest as she backed away. Without another word, another glance, she got in her car and drove away. Kent watched her leave, his hand resting on his cheek where she had kissed him, and somehow, he was filled with hope.

AT THE END of the night, Jeddie took a moment to herself and climbed into the tree house as the sun set over the valley. She swung her legs over the edge of the balcony and stared at the envelope Lisa had given her that afternoon. She bit her lip, debating whether or not to open it, to find out what Lisa could possibly want to say. Then, making sure she was alone, she broke the seal and pulled out the letter.

Inside the folds was a black-and-white photo. On the back, it read *Jeddie 9 months*. It was the same handwriting she had seen on the picture frame in Peter's room. In the photo, Lisa was giving Jeddie a kiss on the cheek, and Jeddie's whole face was lit up, her smile open wide. Seeing the picture, Jeddie smiled, tears flooding her vision. It was the first time she had seen proof that, at some point, Lisa had loved her.

Jeddie blinked, clearing her vision so she could read, then puffed her cheeks and blew her hair out of her face. Her hands trembled as she lifted the folds of the paper and began to read.

*JEDDIE,*

*My sweet girl, you are so grown up. There are so many things I wish I could say to you, but none of them seem adequate enough to express how sorry I am. The truth is, I never meant to hurt you. I made an excuse for a long time that everything I did was to protect Peter, but in reality, I never healed after losing you. So I took drastic steps to protect myself, to prevent the possibility of being hurt again, and in turn, I ended up being so ashamed by what I had done that I never wanted you to know me. Shame is a powerful feeling and I let it consume me. I never want you to be like me, not this version of me...*

*Your dad is right about you. You are a beautiful, determined, driven girl. You have so much to give the world, and I don't want you to be dragged down by me. I'm going to work hard to change and when that happens, if you'll still accept me, I'll come running. Until we meet again, my sweet girl.*

*Love,*
*Mom*

JEDDIE LET her tears splash the page as they rolled off her cheeks. The letter didn't exactly make her feel better about the whole situation, but she could see that Lisa was trying, and that meant a lot. She closed the letter as she heard someone behind her.

"Hey, you okay?" It was Peter.

"I will be," she said, nodding.

Peter walked to the edge and dangled his feet off the side. Jeddie looked at him in surprise. "How did you get to be so brave?"

"Must be something in the air," he joked. "But really, I feel totally different this week. You know what I mean?"

"Yeah, I think I do." Jeddie smiled up at him then rested her head on his shoulder.

"Speaking of which, there's something I want to show you."

"What's that?"

"Lakewood."

Jeddie lifted her head off his shoulder and looked at him, puzzled. "You want to go back there?"

"Just for the day. Tomorrow?"

"Sure," Jeddie answered, still totally perplexed.

THE NEXT DAY, Kent, Jeddie, and Peter stood at the front doors of Lakewood. Peter was second-guessing his decision to come back.

"We don't have to do this, Peter," Jeddie said behind him.

"I know. But I want to."

He pressed the door buzzer, and Margie's voice projected through the intercom. "Peter? What are you doing here?"

"Hey, Margie. Do you mind if we come in?"

"Not at all."

The doors clicked opened and they walked to the reception desk.

"I was wondering if I could show the two of them around."

"Yeah, you bet."

Peter looked at her, surprised. He wasn't sure if she would let him.

"Thanks," he said, walking down the hallway. He motioned Jeddie and Kent to follow. Peter opened the door to his bedroom. Everything was just as he had left it. The posters on his wall, his bed neatly made, even the baseball was on his bed. "This is where I grew up," Peter said to Kent and Jeddie.

He turned around to see both of them pinned in the

entryway, shocked looks on their faces. Both of them looked around the room, seemingly taking it all in, not saying a word.

Jeddie finally took another step in the room. "You lived in here?"

Peter sensed the disgust in her voice. "Yeah...for seven long years."

Jeddie, seemingly noticing a few white marks on the wall, walked over to the bedframe and pulled it away for the wall. White tally marks covered every inch of the wall behind his bed. Peter walked over to her.

"I went through a bit of a rough phase. Once I realized we wouldn't be leaving Lakewood, I started counting how many days we stayed here. I think this started about my second year."

Jeddie looked at Kent, who was backing out of the room. "I...uh...I don't think I should be here." His voice broke. He hurried back down the hallway heading for the exit.

"Is he okay?" Peter asked.

"I don't think it's easy for him to see this. He blames himself for what you went through."

"Well, I don't. I thought that bringing you both here would be a good thing. You could see that it wasn't *so bad*." Saying it out loud made him realize his mistake. It sounded like he was trying to convince himself it wasn't bad. If he couldn't convince himself, how was he ever supposed to convince them?

"It's pretty bad, Peter." Lightening the mood, she gave him a wry smile. "Come on, let's go."

He gave Margie a sad wave on their way out. Kent was waiting on the side lawn for them, looking out at the lake.

"I'm so sorry," Peter said.

"No, Peter, don't apologize. Everything is still sinking in, and I just don't think I was quite ready to see that."

"I get that. But please know I don't blame you. There was nothing you could have done."

"I'm working on believing that."

"If anything, this was actually good for me," Peter relaxed his shoulders, looking up at the barred windows. "This place doesn't seem so scary anymore."

Kent pulled both Jeddie and Peter into a hug, squeezing tight. "All right, you two, let's get going. I believe you still have a class project to finish."

Two weeks later, Mr. Jensen called Peter and Jeddie to the front of the class to give their presentation. They looked at each other and smiled, jumping out of their seats. Besides Natalie, they hadn't told anyone at school what had happened, so they could only imagine how their classmates were going to react when they told them they were twins. Kent and Elaine stood in the back of the room to show their support, waiting in anticipation.

"Our project turned out to be nothing like we had ever expected," Jeddie said.

Then, Peter added, "It all started with a house fire seven years ago..."

# THANK YOU FOR READING MY BOOK!

PLEASE LEAVE A REVIEW ON AMAZON. EACH REVIEW HELPS MY BOOK GET DISCOVERED BY OTHER READERS. I WOULD BE EXTREMEMLY GRATEFUL IF YOU WOULD TAKE A FEW MINUTES TO LEAVE A REVIEW.

IF YOU LIKED THIS BOOK, SHARE ON SOCIAL MEDIA USING THE HASHTAG #THEFIREESCAPEBOOK

I AM GRATEFUL FOR ALL OF MY READERS, SO AGAIN, THANK YOU SO MUCH FOR BEING A PART OF THIS JOURNEY!

-WHITNEY

HTTP://WWW.LIVINGTHEWRITEWAY.COM

instagram.com/whitney.johnson.writes

Made in the USA
Monee, IL
09 February 2021